ENCOUNTER OVER ALASKA

MARK BARRESI

CALUMET EDITIONS
Minneapolis

**CALUMET
EDITIONS**
Minneapolis, Minnesota

SECOND EDITION DECEMBER 2022

This is a work of fiction. All of the characters, names, incidents, organizations, and dialogue are either the products of the author's imagination or are used fictiously.

10 9 8 7 6 5 4 3 2

ISBN: 978-1-959770-96-1
Cover and book design by Gary Lindberg

EXCITEMENT FOR
ENCOUNTER OVER ALASKA

"I'm excited about transforming the book *Encounter Over Alaska* into a major motion picture, and my company, Saturn Harvest, LLC, is well on the way towards that end. While I have been involved in many exceptional films, including Winter's Tale with Colin Farrell and M. Night Shyamalan's *The Visit*, I have always been drawn to films exploring the unknown. The story behind *Encounter Over Alaska* is exceptional. The JAL 1628 incident is the best documented alien encounter of all time, and the most well-known UFO event outside of Roswell."

If you look at the most popular films in theaters, such as *Avengers: Endgame* to *X-Men*, all of them draw from UFO mythology. And this is hardly a new phenomenon, as directors like Stephen Spielberg and James Cameron have made careers telling stories based on extraterrestrial lore. There is an enduring, worldwide fascination with the UFO phenomenon, and *Encounter Over Alaska* dives deep into the mystery that captivates the world."

Brandon Blake
Producer and CEO
Saturn Harvest, LLC

"If you think UFOs are small, distant lights, and if you think they're never seen by reliable witnesses like airline pilots, and never tracked on radar, then think again. The phrase "based on true events" is overused these days, but in this case, it's true. While *Encounter over Alaska* is a work of fiction, the central event from which this book takes its inspiration really happened. It's one of the most spectacular and disturbing UFO incidents of all time—and it remains unexplained to this day."

Nick Pope
UK Ministry of Defence UFO Project (Ret.)

ENCOUNTER OVER ALASKA

MARK BARRESI

PREFACE

On November 17, 1986, flight JAL 1628 cargo jet made international history. The routine flight encountered three massive UFOs while the crew was on its way to land at Anchorage, Alaska. Days after the incident happened, it became one of the most famous UFO cases of all time. This is what Encounter over Alaska is based on. When lead executive investigator for accidents and incidents for the Federal Aviation Administration, Scott Andrews, is made aware of the case, he is at first unfazed by the report and believes there must be a plausible reason for the experienced pilot and his crew to have made up such a claim about UFOs over Alaska. But when investigative reporter, Nicole Martone, proves to Andrews there is a cover-up of evidence—of both military and civilian radar reports of the UFOs tracking the 747 cargo plane for over forty-five minutes—together, Andrews and Martone will fight to put all the pieces together and find out why FAA officials and even the CIA would cover up this incident. Scott will not only risk his career but also his own life, as he fights to prove to the world that one of the most famous UFO cases since the Roswell Incident did, indeed, take place. Get ready for an unbelievable thrill ride, as one man fights to seek the truth and the answer to the biggest question of all time and share what he finds with the whole world. Are we truly alone in the universe? One of the most debated and controversial subjects of all time is brought to light in this adrenaline-filled novel by Mark Barresi.

THE BEGINNING

Japan cargo jet, JAL 1628, had just left Keflavík, Iceland, on its way to refuel again at Anchorage, Alaska. It was October 17, 2010. The 747 cargo plane had just finished its first leg of the journey back home to Japan. The flight had begun in Paris, France, where the three-man crew, headed by captain Joe Hiroki, had picked up its cargo of many cases of Bijele wine before starting the return trip to Tokyo, Japan. Captain Hiroki planned the return flight to follow the polar flight route—high above Europe, taking them over Greenland and into Canada. They were to stop at Ted Stevens Airport in Anchorage to refuel a second time before they set out on their final journey home to Tokyo. The plane was now cruising at 35,000 feet, cruise altitude, as they passed over Canada into Alaskan airspace. At 5:11 p.m., Captain Hiroki and his copilot, Ryo Makoto, noticed an unusual set of lights in a square pattern 2,000 feet below them to their ten o'clock position. Hiroki watched this strange pattern of lights for a few moments, as he thought they might be in the trail of American fighter planes. Eielson Air Force Base was only four hundred miles due east of their position. As pilot and copilot continued to watch the two sets of lights, something bizarre happened. The lights very quickly went from the ten o'clock position to the twelve o'clock position and back to the ten o'clock position again very quickly. *No modern plane can move at this speed from left to right*, thought Hiroki. He expressed the thought to his copilot, who agreed with him. Hiroki should know about many planes and their capability as he had twenty-nine years of flight experience.

As the two men continued to talk about the lights, Flight Engineer Sora Takumi, who was seated behind them, also watched in amazement of the lights quick change of flight positions. Hiroki quickly radioed the air traffic control tower in Anchorage to confirm whether they had any known traffic in their area. The controller told them, "No known traffic." All of a sudden, the lights quickly shot straight up to the jet's windshield and stopped only about five hundred feet in front of them. The lights shone so brightly they almost blinded the whole crew, who stood viewing the amazing but horrific display right in front of their eyes. Two cylinder-shaped crafts with portals of many holes from which orange and yellow flames shot exhaust moved from side to side. One was high above and the other below, and the crafts moved simultaneously with one another. They kept pace with the jet, matching its speed of 600 mph. The crew was now very scared. Captain Hiroki noted that the crafts were as big as two DC-10 planes. He quickly radioed back to Stevens Tower to inform the controllers of what the crew was encountering.

> JAL:
> JAL to AATCC, any known traffic at our twelve o'clock position?
>
> AATCC:
> JAL, no known traffic at your twelve o'clock flight space.
>
> JAL:

We have formation of crafts with white and yellow
strobe lights making unknown movements in our
flight path.

AATCC:
JAL, can you distinguish the type of aircraft? Can
you tell if it's military or civilian?

JAL:
Ah, we cannot identify the type. It is quite big… ah,
it is quite big. Like in formation, formation.

Just then, the air tower in Anchorage received an urgent
message from Eielson AFB confirming that a target of an unknown
object was in trail of flight 1628. The controller quickly radioed
back to Hiroki to confirm that there was a target on their radar of
unknown traffic following the flight.

Copilot Makato checked the plane's radar, and it also showed
an object in trail. Hiroki continued to look at the two UFOs, and the
intense glow of the lights made his face feel warm. All of a sudden,
the two crafts rose up to the left a few thousand feet away from the
jet and disappeared behind them. As Hiroki and his crew looked
around to see if they could spot the UFOs again, Hiroki radioed
back to Anchorage tower to confirm that the unknown traffic had
disappeared from their airspace.

Just then, Eielson AFB radioed Anchorage tower again, this
time to confirm the flight size of two and that the crafts were
following their primary target—JAL 1628. The controllers use of
the term "flight size of two" meant that an unknown object was
in trail of the jet for unknown reasons and that they may have
to scramble military jets to intercept the UFOs before they took
hostile actions against the civilian cargo jet.

Hiroki saw the lights of the city of Fairbanks just a few hundred miles ahead of them. He looked to his eight o'clock position and was shocked beyond belief at what his eyes fixed on. A massive ship shaped like a shelled walnut, with yellow lights running all around it, was now in trail of the cargo jet. Hiroki noted to himself that the UFO was twice the size of an American aircraft carrier. He quickly radioed back to Anchorage tower to ask permission to change their flight path—to get away from the enormous UFO.

JAL:
Request heading two four zero.

AATCC:
JAL, request given as necessary for traffic.

JAL:
Ah, it's a very big object!

Captain Hiroki quickly dialed the new heading into the autopilot. The jet made a 360-degree turn; Hiroki hoped this would allow them to get away from the huge UFO. The jet now sped up to its new speed of 700 mph and began to turn to the right. Hiroki noticed that the huge UFO had matched their speed and was fixed only a few thousand feet from their left wing tip. The jet completed the turn and settled on its new path, preparing to land at Stevens Airport soon. The crew looked around to see if they could find the UFO. The object still showed up on their radar, in trail of their position.

Anchorage tower asked United flight 69 to change its flight path and fly in position of 1628, to confirm any unknown object trailing the latter. It had been over forty-five minutes and 600 miles since the cargo jet had first encountered the strange objects high above Alaskan airspace.

Copilot Makato informed Hiroki that the object had gone off their radar screen. Hiroki looked out around them to his right and left, wondering if they had gotten away from the UFOs.

Just then, flight 69 radioed Anchorage tower.

UNT 69:
Be advised, we are viewing JAL1628 about 4,000
degrees to our twelve o'clock. We don't see any
known traffic in trail or in their airspace, Anchorage.

AATCC:
UNT 69, do you confirm? No known traffic in trail of
JAL1628?

UNT 69:
That is confirmed. Their plane is silhouetted against a
light sky, and no traffic in their airspace.

AATCC:
UNT 69, thank you. You may proceed back to
original course of heading.

AATCC:
JAL, you are now cleared for landing at Anchorage.

JAL:
AATCC, thank you.

Captain Hiroki set his landing gear to land, as he viewed Ted Stevens's beacon lights guiding the jet to the landing lane. Hiroki, Makoto, and Takumi looked at one another and smiled; they also shared a very big sigh of relief. While they were relieved that they would be able to land safely at Anchorage, they still didn't know what they had seen or, most of all, why they'd encountered the three huge UFOs. As their plane came to rest at the far runway, Anchorage tower radioed Hiroki, requesting he and his crew come to the tower right away to brief them on what had just transpired.

Hiroki radioed back, "Understood."

CHAPTER 1

It was Tuesday morning, October 18. The alarm clock was going off very loudly as Scott Andrews awoke, reached over, and shut it off. He glanced at the time on the clock's digital face. It read 5:30 a.m. Scott very slowly sat up in bed, starting to stretch and loosen his tense muscles in his back and legs. He thought back to his days in the air force, to waking up early for PT and running three to five miles with his platoon. Now he just liked to lift weights and kickbox to stay in shape.

Scott was the head executive manager for the division of accidents and investigations for the Federal Aviation Administration. He'd spent seven years in the air force as a chief mechanic supervisor, investigating plane failures and accidents. He'd retired at the rank of technical sergeant and had been with the FAA ever since. He had been in his current position for seven years now—a very high accomplishment, given that he was still only forty-one years old.

Scott was tall and broad-shouldered, due to his dedication to kickboxing and weightlifting at his favorite gym near his condo in Brentwood, just outside of Washington, DC, where he worked at the head office.

Scott turned on his cell phone, taking it with him into the bathroom to shave and shower. He had to hurry to pick up his daughter and take her to school, as she lived with Scott's ex-wife in the upscale suburbs of Stoney Brook Estates. Scott got his shaving gear ready and splashed hot water onto his face to wake himself up. He heard the voice on his messaging service tell him he had three new messages. "Way to start the day," he muttered to himself.

He listened to the first message from the office in Alaska, instructing him to call them immediately about an incident they'd had with a cargo jet last night. Scott thought to himself that there may have been something wrong with the plane itself. Or perhaps a bird had struck the plane, given that bald eagles and other large birds were very common in the Alaskan skies.

He quickly listened to the next message; his ex-wife, Kim, reminded him to hurry up this morning—that he had to take their daughter to chorus practice early before regular class started. Scott frowned into the mirror at himself as he began to shave. *Why can't she call me the night before to tell me this?*

He hurried to shave and hop in the shower as he listened to the final message. His executive assistant, Susan Morrow, told him they needed to meet with the head administrator once he got into his office this morning. Scott now knew something very serious must have happened last night with that cargo jet. Only something big would require him to meet with FAA administrator Stephen Clayton first thing in the morning.

***

It was just ten minutes till 7:00 a.m. when Scott pulled up outside Kimberly's nice townhouse. He honked the horn loudly and muttered, "Too bad if she's mad that I'm early to pick up Alex."

He called Susan on her cell phone to tell her he'd be at the office a little before 8:00 a.m. Susan told him she'd wait for him.

As Scott hung up, Kimberly came out of the house, wearing her long bathrobe with a mad face on. *Here we go!* Scott said to himself.

"What are you doing here so early? I said she needed to be at chorus early, but she can still wait like twenty minutes," Kim informed him.

Scott told her he had no time—that he had an important meeting at work and needed to get going now. Alexandra came running out of the house with her book bag and got into the passenger seat of Scott's blue Honda Accord. Alex kissed Scott on the cheek then rolled the window down to talk to her mother. Kim told her to have fun at chorus and have a great day at school, that she would see her this evening when she got home from work. She kissed Alex on the cheek, and Scott rolled up the window and made a smile at Kim as he drove away quickly.

* * *

Kim stood there in the cool breeze of the early morning, thinking to herself, *If it wasn't for Alexandra, I wish I had nothing left to do with him!*

* * *

As Scott pulled onto the main road and headed toward Alex's school, Alex wondered what the serious look on her father's face was about. He looked straight out at the road ahead.

"Dad, are you okay? You look so serious and mad for some reason."

Scott just looked over at Alex and broke into a smile. "I'm fine. It's just that I have to hurry and get to work for an important meeting this morning. That's why I came a little early to pick you up. I'm sorry, honey."

"No. It's all right. I understand. I just wish you and Mom could get along better at times. I wish we could be a family again," Alexandra told her father with a sad look in her eyes.

Scott glanced at her and quickly looked back at the road. He knew his divorce from Kim going on four years ago was hard on Alex. But he also knew that it was best for Kim to move on, as Scott would travel up to weeks on end all over the country and overseas, whenever problems occurred with American planes. "Look, Alex, I know how you must feel about your mother and me not being together anymore. But it was the best thing for her and you. My job takes me away from you both many hours of the day, and we have to spend too many days apart when I have to go away. Your mother can move on and find another nice man to be with. And very soon you'll be on to college next year. So it will work out for all of us in the end.

Alex just frowned and said, "I guess so."

Scott pulled up to the school, and Alex opened the door. She kissed her father and told him she loved him. She closed the door and ran to meet her friends, walking up the stairs with them toward the main entrance.

"Yeah I guess so too," Scott said to himself quietly, as he pulled out and drove toward his office.

***

Unlocking the door, Scott entered his office. He quickly sat behind his large desk and called the Alaskan FAA office. Scott took out a long sheet of paper and a pen, ready to take notes. He was connected to the shift supervisor on duty at the time of the incident. The supervisor filled Scott in on what had happened with the Japanese cargo jet. He asked Scott what they should tell the media about the plane encountering the UFOs.

Dumbstruck at hearing the word *UFOs*, Scott didn't reply immediately. Susan knocked on his door and quietly came into his office, and Scott motioned for her to take a seat. She sat down facing him. Scott listened to the supervisor, who was now explaining that the plane had landed safely in Anchorage and refueled and was now on its way back to Japan.

Scott contemplated what to tell the media about the incident. "Look, tell the reporters that the Japanese plane landed safely at Anchorage. Say that the pilot and his crew mistook the bright rays of the moon as an unknown object." Scott told the supervisor not to say the word *UFO* in his statement to the press. He knew doing so would cause panic among the public. Susan nodded her head, indicating that she agrees with the way Scott was handling the situation.

When he hung up the phone, Susan informed him that they were to meet with their boss, Stephen Clayton, in a half hour to discuss the incident.

"What a way to start a morning—UFOs; a big meeting with Clayton; and to top it all off, I may have to fly up to Alaska about this," Scott said, laughing.

Susan told him she'd get her folder and list of contacts in the Alaskan office so that Scott could begin to debrief them.

***

As Scott and Susan entered Mr. Clayton's large office, he instructed them to sit at his round conference table. He was still on the phone talking to someone in a very soft tone, ensuring his conversation would not be overheard.

Scott and Sue noticed a large LCD projection map screen that showed a view of the whole state of Alaska and half of western Canada. A red line marked the plane's flight path over the Yukon

Territory, crossing into Alaska over the city of Fairbanks. Scott and Susan noted to each other the large circle that marked the screen just east of Fairbanks.

Clayton got off the phone and came over to the large table with a folder in his hand, taking a seat. He explained the flight plan of JAL 1628; it began in Paris, with two scheduled stops in Iceland and Anchorage to refuel, before heading home to Tokyo. Clayton pointed to the screen, showing the first point of contact—the spot where the pilot had first claimed to encounter the UFOs. Then Clayton pointed out the circle just over Fairbanks, marking the exact point where the crew then claimed they viewed the massive object and asked the Anchorage tower for permission to change course. From this spot, JAL 1628 had made its 360-degree turn.

Scott asked what his function in the investigation would be.

"Scott, I want you to fly up to Anchorage and talk with the controllers who were in contact with the flight crew until the plane landed," Clayton replied. "I want to know exactly what was said between them and the pilots. My guess is that this is all nothing, that these guys may have opened one of the bottles of French wine they were boarding."

The trio laughed, and Scott told his boss he understood his task.

"Sue, this was already leaked to the media in Anchorage in the context of UFOs. I instructed our public relations office there to tell the media that the pilots mistook the full moon as an unknown large object in the sky. I want you to make the same report to the media here until we can sort this all out."

Both Scott and Susan acknowledged their assignments, and Scott asked when he was leaving for Anchorage.

Clayton smiled and said, "This evening."

Scott just smiled and said he understood, as he cursed himself, not wanting to fly all the way up to Alaska.

As Scott and Susan walked quickly to the elevators to take them back to their floor, Scott instructed her to monitor all his calls and e-mails while he was gone. Scott told her he would be making copies of the voice tapes and instructing the tech office to make copies of the plane's entire flight plan and radar hits over Alaska, in hopes of pinpointing any unknown aircraft in the cargo jet's flight space. Susan told Scott she would get right on it.

Scott quickly went into his office and started to get some of his investigation files ready to begin the case.

He called Kimberly on her cell phone to tell her he would be away for a while. She told him she was not happy that he would, once again, be far away from their daughter in the event that something happened and hung up on him.

"What else is new with her?" Scott muttered.

He called Dulles Airport to confirm his flight to Alaska for 9:00 p.m. He spoke with a guest service agent and confirmed his flight then left for home to pack a suitcase.

***

Stephen Clayton was still busy working in his office past 5:00 p.m., when his desk phone rang and caller ID displayed a DC area code.

Clayton answered and was stunned when the person on the other line introduced himself as a CIA agent. He went over all the key findings regarding the pilot's claims and the radar findings. The agent then instructed Clayton on how the CIA wanted the FAA to handle the case from this point on. The agent, Carlos Dorey, explained to Clayton that the FAA was no longer to discuss this case with the media or anyone else in Clayton's top staff. Dorey explained that there would be an emergency meeting with himself and a few other agents from the CIA, along with the members of the president's scientific staff and that the group would join the FAA's investigative team tomorrow at 10:00 a.m. in the FAA's boardroom. Clayton told Dorey that lead investigator Scott Andrews was inbound for Alaska as they spoke to begin his investigation into the case. Dorey acknowledged Andrews's investigation, telling Clayton that he had agents already in Anchorage to begin the shutdown of the events.

CHAPTER 2

It was late, past 11:00 p.m., when Scott arrived in Anchorage, Alaska. He was met at Ted Stevens Airport by other FAA officials, who let him settle into a nearby hotel. They told him he would soon meet with the control tower crew that was in contact with the cargo jet at the time of the event.

Scott had a quick dinner with the FAA officials before returning to his room to get some sleep. He called his daughter to let her know he was fine and reassured her that he would be home soon to take her to the upcoming DC festival. As he got off the phone with Alexandra, he lay down on the bed. He looked out the window at the dark blue skies of Alaska, smiled, and thought, *UFOs*. He was curious to know what would make the flight crew make up a story like that. Scott closed his eyes and fell asleep.

***

Early the next morning, Scott was up, shaved, and showered in time to be picked up and brought back to the very large and busy airport. Scott had his laptop computer, along with his flight incident report files, in hand. He was ready to record the testimonies of the control tower crew. Upon being led into a conference room, he saw two men he didn't know. Also, there was the FAA's field office investigator for Anchorage, Bill Turner, whom Scott had known for some time.

Turner introduced the others. The lead controller for the shift and the person who was in constant contact with flight 1628 was Thom Brown. Seated next to Brown was his navigation assistant, Sean Thomas. Thomas shook Scott's hand in a friendly manner, but he had a very serious and still look on his face. The expression gave Scott the impression that this guy already knew what he wanted to say and that he wanted to get this over with.

Scott took a seat with the men around the large, square table. He readied his computer and documents and began asking the two men questions, starting with the exact time and location they first received transmission from the flight crew of JAL 1628.

Brown told Scott that it was 5:11 p.m. their time when the pilot first contacted the tower about traffic in their area. Brown went on to say that this was when the pilots first saw they had traffic in their air space on the 747's radar, which told them the traffic was 2,000 feet below and positioned at their ten o'clock heading. Sean Thomas told Scott the crew members could have picked up an echo of their own plane's image on both the 747's radar and the tower radar. Scott nodded, saying that could be possible given the proximity of the Brooks Range mountains, as the high peaks could interfere, making an echo image of their own on the radars. Brown just smirked.

Scott then asked the two men how the flight crew had described the UFOs in terms of appearance. Brown told Scott about the crafts having white and yellow strobe lights, as Turner showed Scott the transcript of the radio conversation between the tower and pilots at the time.

Scott read it over to himself then looked up at Turner, stunned. He pointed out, "Nowhere in this transcript is there any mention of UFOs or unknown crafts. It just reads that the pilots asked the tower if they had any known traffic in their airspace."

Thomas pointed out that, at the same time the Japan cargo jet entered Alaskan airspace, two F-16 Fighting Falcon jets were returning to Eielson Air Force Base. The crew aboard 1628 would have gotten the very bright glare of the fighter jet's rear lights and flames. In the dark Alaskan sky, it would have made any pilot question what he or she was looking at when at an altitude of 35,000 feet.

Scott then looked at the flight chart copy, which showed the number of planes and their tail numbers to identify them, showing what planes were in the air at that time of night. Bill Turner highlighted the two F-16s in the airspace of flight 1628. Scott shook his head and looked up with a convinced look on his face. The three men told Scott that the Japanese crew had made an honest mistake; maybe the crew's lack of familiarity with Alaska's dark skies and bright northern lights had contributed. The aurora's bright rays seen at the middle to northern Alaskan skies would amaze and stun any pilot who was seeing them for the first time. As Turner pointed out, this was the first flight Joe Hiroki had ever made into Alaska.

Scott looked at the clock on the wall. They'd been going over this for about an hour now. He was pleased that he had enough to make out an adequate incident report to return to Clayton. The report would confirm that JAL 1628's flight crew had made an honest mistake in its report of unknown crafts. Scott gathered his things together and stored his computer in its carrying case. He shook all the men's hands and thanked them for their full cooperation for his report. Turner informed Scott he would catch up to him in a few minutes, and Scott left the conference room.

***

Sean Thomas waited for a couple of minutes before he spoke. "That was a very good job you both did convincing Mr. Andrews this was but an honest mistake made by those pilots," he said as he gathered up the incorrect flight chart and transcripts of the conversation between the pilots and the control tower.

Turner looked at Thomas. "So the media and, most of all, the public will never know of this incident, will they?" he asked.

"Mr. Turner, my job is to make certain this incident is stopped here and now. I did not like having to make you both lie to Scott Andrews, but he and all the other investigators are not to be told that this incident really took place. There are good reasons why we have to hide things from the honest public, and the reality of UFOs and life elsewhere in the universe is one of those things. Thank you, gentlemen." With that, CIA Agent Sean Thomas gathered the files and left the room.

Both Turner and Thom Brown knew they couldn't speak of what had really happened to Andrews or anyone else from this point on.

***

The meeting in the FAA boardroom was now going into its third hour. It was just after noon eastern standard time. Susan Morrow was seated next to Stephen Clayton, as CIA Agent Carlos Dorey briefed the whole group, with two other CIA agents, along with three scientists from the president's scientific staff.

Dorey pointed to the large projection screen behind him, which showed the recorded radar movements of the cargo jet and the three UFOs. Dorey then asked for one of the scientists to speak out on the movements of the UFOs.

The scientist, a doctor in the field of advanced aircraft propulsion systems, explained to the whole group, "The UFOs move from six to ten miles around the cargo jet from its ten o'clock position then very quickly to twelve miles behind the jet at its eight o'clock position." He admitted that there was no known propulsion system in NASA's or the air force's known aircraft capable of duplicating these kinds of speeds. He admitted that military scientists were experimenting with nuclear fusion propulsion jet engines at Los Alamos science labs in New Mexico. But that had not been able to produce these kinds of results at the current time.

Susan, stunned by the findings, whispered to Clayton, "We need to tell Scott about this."

Clayton shook his head, indicating that she should remain silent.

Agent Dorey played the recorded voice tapes for all to hear, simultaneously replaying the radar scope of the jets movements from the first contact with the UFOs, as the jet just entered Alaskan airspace. The radar and cockpit recordings of the pilots confirmed the presence of the UFOs.

Dorey told the group, "This is the first time we have ever received radar confirmation of UFOs on both military and civilian radar. We will be confiscating all the voice tapes and radar recordings, along with the printout of the cargo jet's flight path.

Susan looks up stunned and asked him why, saying that they needed to tell the public about this. Everyone in the room looked at Susan, and Clayton told her to be quiet.

Carlos Dorey stared at her for a few seconds before he answered her. "No, Miss Morrow, we will not tell the public, or anyone else, about this incident. If we go around telling our nation and the nations of the world that we have confirmation of alien contact from other planets, it will cause panic among the public. We have been keeping a lid on this subject ever since the Roswell Incident of July 1947. Now we will take all this evidence and analyze it back at CIA headquarters and Los Alamos National Laboratory. If our scientists can duplicate this kind of propulsion and craft design, it will put our national defense light years beyond other countries' capabilities.

"None of this is to be mentioned again, and you are all sworn to secrecy as oaths to your country. Do I make myself clear everyone?!" Dorey raised his voice as he spoke the last sentence, directing a very unfriendly stare at Susan. He needed to be certain she would not speak out to anyone about this. Dorey continued to explain how the cover-up story would go—the cargo jet was in trail of two US Air Force fighter jets and mistook their rear lights and engine flames as unknown objects. He said that they needed to move quickly on this, as pilot Joe Hiroki had already talked to the Japanese media about seeing UFOs on his flight over Alaska. Dorey asked Clayton if he had everything, and Clayton told him he had all the copies made of everything and that this incident would not be spoken of again by any of his people.

"Very good, Mr. Clayton. Now if you would excuse me, I need to brief the CIA director of this, as well as the president."

Dorey left with his agents and the three scientists, leaving Susan standing next to Clayton in shock. Stephen again reminded her not to mention this to Scott or anyone else in the FAA departments. Susan very softly told him that she understood and left the boardroom, hurrying back to her office.

***

As she closed and locked the door behind her, Susan contemplated what to do. She wanted to tell Scott about what had happened, and she knew that Agent Dorey may have already put the same cover story out to hide this from Scott. She also knew that she couldn't tell him herself; she couldn't get involved directly.

She took out her cell phone and called a friend of hers.

"Hello, Susan," answered the very friendly voice.

"Nicole, look, I don't have much time to explain this all to you now. But you know my boss, Scott Andrews?"

"Yes, I know him," Nicole answered.

"There is going to be big news about a UFO sighting from Alaska, which happened on the seventeenth. Hurry and write down all I tell you, and then you have to contact Scott right away. He'll get back to town tomorrow." Susan told her good friend, Nicole Martone, all about the incident in Alaska and the cover-up by the CIA. She instructed Nicole that she had to be the one to convince Scott of this and then tell the public. Nicole Martone was an investigative reporter for *The Washington Times*.

***

Friday morning, October 21, started as usual for Scott. He dropped off Alexandra at school and promised to spend some time with her over the coming weekend then made his way into his office. He called Clayton at his extension to tell him he had the incident report ready. Clayton informed Scott that he would pass by Scott's office to get it from him soon.

As Scott just hung up the phone, there was a knock on his door and Susan entered, a glum look on her face. She greeted him, and Scott asked her what was wrong.

"So, did you find out what was the cause of the UFO sighting that night?" she asked him.

"Yes," he replied. "The 747 jet was in trail of two F-16 fighter jets from nearby Eielson Air Force Base. The pilots mistook their rear lights and afterburners as unknown traffic, and the moon was full and very bright that night. When you combine the two elements, you have pilots unfamiliar with the Alaskan skies believing they are seeing UFOs." Scott explained the plane's own echo as the reason there was radar confirmation of an unknown object.

"That's what we understood here in a briefing held by Clayton yesterday."

Scott looked at her, confused, and asked how Clayton would know that when Scott hadn't had a chance to tell him of his findings with the control tower operators at the time.

"Please, Scott, just listen to me. I can't tell you anything about what was said in the briefing. But you have to talk to this reporter for me." Susan handed Scott a small piece of paper with Nicole's contact information and stated who Nicole was.

Scott shot Susan a shocked look and asked her why he had to speak to a reporter about this case when Stephen himself was holding a news conference this afternoon to explain to the public that the "sighting" had been a pilot's honest error.

"Please, Scott! Trust me on this. I wish I could tell you, but I can't. Nicole wants you to call her today and meet with her this evening. She lives very close to you." Susan tried to convince Scott to meet with Nicole.

Scott reads the reporter's full name and cell phone number, looks up at Susan and smiled. "Fine," he told her. "I will talk to this young lady for you, only if she is good looking!"

Scott was only kidding, and Susan laughed out loud. She smiled back at him and told him about Nicole. "Scott, Nicole Martone is thirty years old and very sharp. So as my friend and boss, please be very pleasant to her."

"I will. I promise you, Sue," Scott replied with a smile and a wink.

Susan started to head for the door. Then she looked back. "Oh and, Scott, Nicole is very good looking." She winked and left his office.

Scott dialed Nicole's cell number.

As Scott was talking to Nicole about a time and place to meet that evening, Stephen Clayton knocked on his door and walked in.

"Okay, 8:00 p.m.; see you then," he said and hung up.

Clayton asked how his trip had gone and whether he'd finished the incident report on the case. Scott handed him all five pages of the report in a folder. Clayton looked through the pages and seemed to be content with Scott's final results. Scott asked him if everything was all right here.

"Everything is fine, Scott. We just had the briefing with our radar tech team yesterday, as they believed the same thing you found. The jet's echo was what showed up on radar as another unknown object, and the pilot mistook the bright full moon as a very large UFO," Clayton said, laughing.

Scott thought to himself, I didn't mention that the pilot claimed he saw "a very large UFO" in my report.

But he just smiled back as Clayton told him he would now get ready to hold the news conference today at noon in the briefing room. He said that Scott and Susan should join him and the other board members to address the media.

CHAPTER 3

Scott waited outside Five Stars Café, as it was just about 8:00 p.m. He had watched the 6:00 p.m. news, as the FAA's news conference was broadcasted all over the local and cable news outlets. According to the report, the recent UFO sighting by a civilian airliner was only a case of misidentification on the part of the pilot and his crew.

Scott looked up and saw a very attractive brunette walk up to him. Nicole introduced herself, and Scott shook her hand, noting that she had a leather portfolio in her other hand ready to take notes. They walked into the café and were seated in the back away from the other patrons, per Nicole's request. The request made Scott felt awkward, but he just went along with her.

They both ordered two cups of coffee, and Nicole asked Scott about the big news conference today and how he felt about it. Scott just shrugged his shoulders and said it had gone well, other than he and his boss, Stephen Clayton, felt embarrassed about having to be involved with a major news story dealing with UFOs.

Nicole stopped smiling and said, "Scott, the incident really happened, and it was covered up by the CIA and FAA. Your boss was told by a head CIA agent to form the cover story explaining away radar confirmations of the multiple UFOs by both the plane and Anchorage tower." Nicole's voice was sharp and firm, and she had a serious look in her eyes.

Scott stared into her eyes for a moment, till he broke a smile and started to laugh at her. "Oh, come on now, Miss Martone! Do you actually believe this to be real—that there are enormous flying objects flying high above the Alaskan tundra? And a 747 cargo plane happens to come in contact with them?"

Scott just laughed as Nicole fired back. "Scott, Susan Morrow contacted me herself to break this news to me. She told me that, during the meeting with Clayton and all the radar specialists the FAA has, CIA agents swore them all to silence and admitted that the radars of both the control tower in Anchorage and Eielson Air Force Base did, indeed, pick up the large UFOs. The agents took all the recorded data and voice tapes from Clayton to study them. I have known Susan for some time, and you know she would not lie about something like this."

Scott just kept staring into Nicole's deep, black eyes. He now had a very serious look on his face. He had known and worked with Susan Morrow for over eight years now, and he knew she would never lie to him about any incident in their investigations together. "Okay, say this is all true? The CIA took all the evidence from us, so how can I prove it now?"

Nicole took out her folder and showed Scott a name she'd written down. Scott remembered the name—Thom Brown. Scott explained to Nicole that Brown was the lead air traffic controller who was in contact with flight 1628 at the time of the incident.

"Scott, Susan spoke to him on the phone right after your meeting with him in Anchorage. Sean Thomas is not an air traffic controller but a CIA agent who was there to start the cover-up. Susan told me Thom Brown made duplicate copies of the black box voice tapes that recorded the conversation between himself in the tower and the plane's pilots. Those tapes confirm the voice communication about the UFOs at the time."

Scott looked around the café to make sure no one could hear their conversation. "In trail of two military jet fighters my ass. We need those tapes, and we need a video copy of the radars if we are going to have a chance to prove this really happened."

"How are we going to do this?" she asked him.

"We are going to have to go back up to Alaska and meet with Thom Brown!" Scott replied.

Nicole nodded her agreement.

"Look, let me make the arrangements to take some time off work, and we can leave together Monday morning for Anchorage. I have to put in for the time off and talk to my ex-wife and daughter. I know Kim is going to be mad at me for not being able to take our daughter to school for the next few days, but she'll have to deal with it." Scott told Nicole they'd have to be in Anchorage for at least a week to talk to Brown and others and gather a lot of information.

Nicole informed him that she'd have to tell her immediate boss that she'd be taking time off to work on a story in Alaska. Then she asked Scott, "Why would you want to help me break this story?"

Scott just shot her a deep stare. "Because I hate being lied to, and I am just as curious and determined to know what happened up there that night as you are."

Nicole smiled back at him, and they finished their coffee.

As they walked to their cars, Scott told her to be very careful and not to mention their motives to anyone, not even Susan. He believed that the CIA may have agents tracking their movements as of now.

***

Back at his condo, Scott got online and made plane reservations for Nicole and him leaving very early Monday morning. He called

Nicole to tell her the flight number and times of their departure from Dulles Airport. Nicole thanked him again for trusting her. Scott warned her that this might get very dangerous for them if there were people willing to go to great lengths to keep the incident quiet. Nicole told Scott that, for this story to come out, she would risk it all to help him uncover the truth. Scott thanked her and called his boss on his cell phone.

"Scott, hi. How are you?" Clayton answered.

Scott said he hoped he wasn't interrupting him, and Stephen told him he'd just finished dinner with his family and now was relaxing watching television. Scott informed his boss he'd be taking the next week off of work to spend time with his daughter and work on projects around his house.

Stephen caught an odd tone in Scott's voice, but he told Scott he could have the time off—that he just needed to inform Susan to cover his desk work and meetings for him. Then his tone grew momentarily serious. "Scott, please, between us—let this go! Don't get involved with this. I don't want you or anyone else to get hurt, understand?" he warned.

"Thanks for the warning, but I have to do what I think is right and honest here. I hope you can understand, boss."

Stephen told him again to be careful as he hung up.

Scott quickly called Susan on her cell to tell her he would be away next week. He said that he'd met with Nicole and that they'd be working together on the case.

"I knew she would be able to convince you, Scott. I just hope we are all doing the right thing here because, like you, I'm not going to lie to anyone about this," Susan told him.

"Hey, we are doing the right thing, and since this all falls on my shoulders, it's up to me to make the truth come out now. And you were right; Nicole is very good looking!" Scott added with a laugh.

"I told you she was. You guys be careful up there, you hear!" she warned.

Scott assured her he would take care of Nicole and asked her to call him if there was a problem at work or with Kim and Alexandra.

Susan told him that she would, of course, call him if something happened.

***

Scott spent most of Saturday and Sunday with Alex. He took her to the mall and out to see two really good movies that were playing.

It was going on 6:00 p.m. Sunday evening, and Scott asked Kim if they could have dinner together at Kim's house, telling her he had some news to tell them. At first, Kim was reluctant to have Scott over for dinner, not knowing what his intentions were. But Alex was very upbeat about the three of them spending time together as a family, so Kim gave into her, and she made a small dinner for the three of them at her house.

At the table, Alexandra told her parents that she was thinking about applying to Princeton and Northwestern University next year. She was excited to be graduating this year from high school. Kim shot Scott a glance to let him know that he'd be the one paying for college.

Scott smiled and told Alex that, if she could pick a good college around here, she wouldn't have to be far away from the family.

Alex laughed and said she would go to Georgetown University to study law instead.

Scott and Kim laughed, and Kim told Alex they will talk about her options when the time came.

Kim looked at Scott and asked, "So, Scott, what's on your mind?" She wanted to know why he'd called to have this dinner together.

"I want to let you both know that I will be away all of next week in Alaska again. I need to do more work for the FAA on this case. It's one of the most complex cases we have ever had to deal with. So I'm sorry, but I won't be able to take Alex to school next week," he told them.

A look of disgust crossed Kim's face. "You know, Scott, you're really something! You know I'm busy at the office doing my own job, and we worked this out between us. You are supposed to take Alexandra to school, and I will be there for when she comes home. You always put your work before her!"

Scott listened to Kim going off on him and then back, stating that there was nothing he could do; it was his job. Both were raising their voices at one another.

Alexandra couldn't take it any longer. "Enough, both of you! I'm not a child anymore, and I'm sick and tired of you both fighting over me. I can take care of myself!" she told them.

Scott and Kim stopped arguing, and Kim held Alex's hand and told her she was sorry. Scott also apologized.

"So, Dad, it must be very important for you to go way back to Alaska for this investigation?" Alex asked him. Kim asked if it had anything to do with the UFO sighting that had been in the news.

Scott told them that, yes, it was a very big matter and that he had to oversee it. Kim pointed out that the sighting must have some truth to it, for him to continue investigating it.

Scott said he couldn't discuss it anymore with them, as it was getting late. He had to go home to finish packing and get some sleep. His plane was to leave at 5:00 a.m. He hugged and kissed Alex on the cheek, and she told him to be very careful and come home soon. He said he would.

Scott asked Kim to talk to him outside for a few minutes. She walked him out onto the front entrance and closed the door behind them so Alex couldn't hear.

"Look, I want you to be very careful while I'm gone. And tell Alex not to mention this to her friends at school, especially through e-mail and on the Internet. Understand me!" Scott said firmly.

Kim said that if the investigation was so dangerous, maybe he shouldn't get involved.

Scott replied that he had to—he had to see this through. "You still have the Glock .45 I got you?" Scott asked.

Kim said that she did—it was in the drawer next to her bed.

"Good. Keep it loaded and ready in case you need it. Understand? I hope you still know how to fire a gun, Kim," he said with a serious look.

"Please, Scott. You forget I was in the military too! Isn't that how we first met, in the air force together?"

Scott smiled. "Yeah, I remember," he said. He gave her Susan's cell phone number and told her to contact Susan if anything bad happened.

Scott kissed Kim gently on the cheek, and she told him to be very careful. Then he heads to his car.

***

When their plane was already four hours into the flight, Scott told Nicole they will be landing in Seattle in two hours.

Nicole asked Scott what they would do when they first arrived in Anchorage. Scott informed her that he wanted them to get settled into their hotel first. He'd made reservations at the Hilton Hotel in downtown Anchorage, not very far from the airport. Nicole asked Scott where they'd meet with Thom Brown, and Scott explained that Susan had texted Brown a message, asking them to meet him at the Whale's Pub. The bar was close to their hotel in the downtown area, and they were to meet Brown after 9:00 p.m., Alaskan time. Scott showed her Brown's cell phone number, which he'd gotten from Susan so she could store it in her BlackBerry. As Nicole saved the number, she took a deep breath and told Scott that she felt like they were on a secret mission in a movie or something. Scott laughed and assured her this was just investigative work they were doing. It would be all right. Nicole whispered that she hoped he was right.

They landed in Anchorage just after 2:00 p.m. and took a taxi over to the Hilton Hotel. Scott requested two rooms on the same floor and close to one another. As they settled into their rooms on the twelfth floor, Scott told Nicole he'd meet her in the lobby for dinner at the hotel restaurant at 6:00 p.m.

Scott unpacking some of his clothes and his laptop computer and sent a quick text message to Susan to let her know that he and Nicole were now in Anchorage and ready to meet with Brown. She texted him back, telling him to be careful.

Scott went over to his window and looked out at Alaska's clear October night. He took in the breathtaking Chugach Mountains in the background and the port overlooking Prince William Sound. Scott wondered what it was about Alaska that a race of aliens from another world would want to investigate. Scott, being former military, would think that a race from another world would be more interested in trying to get advanced knowledge from a country's military might and learn about its scientific and technological capabilities. *Alaska has a few military bases*, he thought, *but it's a very desolate state*. Alaska was far away from other states whose big cities were more densely populated. Scott pondered the point as he got ready to meet Nicole for dinner.

***

As they finished dinner and sipped coffee, Scott instructed Nicole on what he hoped to gain from the conversation with Brown. He explained that he wanted to talk to Brown and get the voice tapes and radar DVD discs as quickly as possible. If all went well, they could view the evidence together right away and make plans to return to DC maybe sooner than they expected.

Scott looked at his watch; it was going on 8:30 p.m. He told Nicole they should get going and signed off on the check for their dinner. They took a taxi over to the Whale's Pub.

CHAPTER 4

Scott saw Thom Brown seated in the rear of the dark, smoky pub. He made a slight wave to Scott and Nicole as they approached the small, round table. Scott introduced Nicole to Brown then got right to the point, asking Brown if he had the items. Brown took out a small paper bag and laid it on the table in front of Scott. Scott very slowly peered inside the bag. He saw a compact disc in its case, as well as a small voice cassette tape that was also cased. Scott closed the bag and handed it over to Nicole. She placed it in her large handbag.

Brown told them that there was another person who could help them on the case even more than he could; the person was a civilian and not connected to the FAA, as he and Scott were. Brown told them the man's name—Ray Walker.

"Scott, he is a retired army veteran and researches all UFO cases, past and present," Brown said. He gave them Walker's cell phone number, stating that Walker lived outside of Anchorage not very far away.

Scott told Nicole they would need to meet with Walker tomorrow. They all got up together to leave the pub, and Scott and Nicole thanked Brown for his cooperation. Nicole asked him if he would help them again if they needed him. He told her of course, adding that he also wanted to see the truth about this important event come out.

As they watched Brown head to the rear parking lot to get his car, Scott called a taxi from his cell phone. He and Nicole would head back to the hotel and go over the evidence they'd just received. Brown pulled out onto the main street and headed west, away from downtown.

***

Two people watched Scott and Nicole get into their taxi. The man who was seated in the passenger seat placed a call on his cell phone.

"Sean, Brown just met with Andrews and the girl. They just left to go back to their hotel. Should we go after them?"

"No, leave Andrews alone for now. Go and find out what information Brown has given them, and keep it quiet as possible," Thomas informed his two agents.

The driver quickly darted out of their parking space to follow Brown to his residence.

***

In Scott's room, he and Nicole viewed the DVD on his laptop. It showed the radar plot of the cargo plane as it entered Alaskan airspace just before 5:00 p.m. on the evening of October 17. Scott used a stopwatch to get the approximate time between when the radar showed up on the disc and the time the pilot and his crew first alerted Anchorage tower that they'd sighted the UFOs.

Nicole slipped the cassette tape into her small tape recorder. The first radio call came over at 5:11 p.m. The pilot spoke in a thick accent, and his exact words were hard to make out. But Scott and Nicole could understand what was being said.

After some time passed, Scott pointed to the screen. A blip showed an unknown object near the plotted plane on the radar screen. The blip disappeared and reappeared around the plane in different locations. Nicole watched the times on the radar screen and the stopwatch. They heard the pilot of United 69 tell Anchorage tower that he didn't see any objects around flight 1628. The radar stopped once the object left the screen. Scott stopped the clock; it read forty-five minutes. He read the mileage on the radar screen when the object vanished. "Four hundred miles," he said. "That's how far the UFOs tracked the 747.

"My God, no wonder they want all this data and keep a major lid on this incident," he told Nicole.

"We have to get back to DC fast, Scott. We can't stay here any longer; I'm sure that if the CIA knows we are here now, they will harm us to get this evidence from us!" Nicole said, clearly very nervous.

He knew she was right. He thought about what to do next then quickly took out the phone number of Ray Walker, the private UFO researcher who Brown had told him about. As Scott punched the number into his cell phone, he told Nicole to hurry up and pack her stuff—that they were leaving immediately.

***

Sean Thomas and his men had followed Thom Brown to his home in the suburb of Kenai, just outside of Anchorage.

Thom was tied up tightly to a chair next to his wife, who was gagged tightly but trying to scream through the heavy duct tape. Tape also bound her legs and feet to her chair. Her husband was similarly bound, but he was not gagged.

Agent Thomas again instructed one of his men to hit Brown in the face hard; blood oozed from Brown's mouth and nose. Thomas yelled again, demanding to know what he had discussed with Scott Andrews and the reporter at the pub.

Brown caught his breath and said, "Nothing."

Thomas smiled and took out a 9 mm pistol that was affixed with a silencer at the barrel. "I'm going to ask you this one last time, Thom. If you don't tell me what was said to the couple or whether you gave them any copies of the radar and voice tapes of what really happened that night, I'm going to kill you and your wife!" he yelled.

As Brown begged Thomas not to hurt him, Thomas smiled and shot him in his left knee. He screamed in pain. Amy screamed and started to cry.

Thomas asked Brown if that had convinced him to talk to them.

Brown cursed Thomas, saying that he would not talk.

Thomas nodded to one of his men, and the man took out a sharp knife and held it under Amy's throat. Thomas vowed that he would have the agent kill Brown's wife if he didn't talk now.

"Okay!" Brown shouted. "Please don't hurt my wife!"

Thomas smiled. "Talk," he commanded.

"I gave them copies of the voice tapes, and a copy of the tower's radar on disc as the UFO tracked the plane. Now please, let us go. I will not tell anyone else of this!"

A mad grin took over Sean Thomas's face. He took out his cell phone and called his boss.

"Carlos, he just admitted to us that he contacted Andrews and the girl. He did make copies of the tape and disc for them. Andrews knows everything now!" Thomas informed his boss. Agent Carlos Dorey was one of the CIA's head agents.

Thomas listened to Dorey's instructions, said he understood and put his phone away in his coat pocket.

"My superior in Washington, DC, wants to thank you for cooperating with us, Mr. Brown, but unfortunately we can't afford to have any witnesses in this case!"

With that, Thomas shot Brown once in his right temple. The blood streamed out of the air traffic controller's head as he closed his eyes.

"Do it!" Thomas told his fellow agent.

The agent slit Amy's throat from ear to ear. As blood gushed out of the open wound, Amy slowly closed her eyes and her head fell down.

"Quickly, get rid of the bodies. We will dump them in Kenai Lake," Sean instructed his men.

As they quickly cut the bodies from the chairs, Thomas placed another call—this one to the two men who were watching Scott and Nicole from a nearby building via a high-powered infrared scope able to see through the thick brick walls of the hotel. The agent who took the call informed Thomas that the couple was gathering their things together to move out now. Thomas instructs the agents to follow them and see where they went, saying that he would catch up to them soon.

***

Scott and Nicole waited in the lobby of the hotel together. Scott looked at the large clock on the wall. It was going on midnight. He looked around at the few people who were in the lobby, wondering if any of them were here to harm them. He looked at Nicole, noting the extreme concern on her face. Holding her right hand, he asked her if she was all right.

Nicole smiled at him. "I am just wondering if my intentions as a reporter didn't put our lives, as well as those of our friends and family, in any danger. I was only doing what I thought was right when Susan called me and told me about all this. I'm sorry, Scott, that I convinced you to get involved." As she finished, she had tears in her eyes.

Scott handed her a clean tissue. "Hey, don't blame yourself, all right. This is my job, first of all. You and Susan did the right thing to make me understand what really happened, and now I want to see this all through. I was taught that always sticking to the truth in life is doing the right thing for all of us!" Scott told her, the anger in his voice evident. He hated that this whole event was to be kept silent and that he had been lied to when he was the chief investigator for the FAA.

Just then, there was a loud honk of a horn. Scott looked out the glass doors to see a large, four-door Toyota Tundra. "That must be him," Scott said.

They walked quickly out the front doors to the gray truck.

Ray Walker rolled down his window and asked, "Scott?"

"Yes," Scott said.

Walker told them to get in quickly, and they loaded their bags into the truck. Scott got into the front passenger seat, and Nicole sat behind Scott. Ray pulled out in a hurry.

***

The two agents waited a few moments and pulled out right behind them.

***

"Both of you make sure your seatbelts are fastened tight!" Ray Walker instructed Scott and Nicole.

"Why?" she asked.

"Because Thom Brown and his wife are dead, and there is a vehicle with CIA agents following us now!" Walker informed them.

Scott and Nicole turned around in their seats, trying to spot the agents' vehicle.

Walker told them to sit still and relax. He had to get out of Anchorage before he could do something about their tail.

Scott asked Ray how he knew that Thom Brown was dead.

"I called him on his cell and home phones several times to let him know I was going to pick you two up tonight. I got no response from him or his wife for the rest of the night. So I know they have been eliminated by agents."

Nicole closed her eyes and prayed silently.

"Whatever Thom told you and whatever items he gave you to confirm this sighting, the CIA doesn't want out. And now they're going to have us eliminated!" Walker said, informing them of the perilous situation they were now facing.

As the truck headed out of Anchorage onto a mountain road, Walker said that he had to lose the agents now. He looked around the two-lane road to see if there was any other traffic around them. Then he floored the gas, quickly speeding up to 80 mph. The smaller, four-door car kept pace with their speed, and Ray kept the vehicle in sight in his rearview mirror. He looked up ahead, knowing he had to be careful in the darkness of night on the Alaskan roads. There were no lampposts to give vehicles light. Only reflecting long rods marked the feet in between the steel barriers off the sides of the highway.

The agents' car sped up, hitting the larger truck from behind.

Nicole screamed in fear, and Ray became angry. "They're trying to force us off the road," Scott said.

Ray smiled and said, "No, they're not!" Then he screamed, "Hold on!" He slammed on the brakes, causing the Tundra to screech its tires hard into the pavement.

The Ford passed them in the other lane. Ray stepped on the gas, and the truck shot forward. Ray raced to catch up to the agents' car. They were soon bumper to bumper with the small car.

One agent tries to aim his pistol out the passenger window to get a shot off. But at these high speeds, the shots missed wildly.

Scott screamed, "What are you going to do?"

Ray smiled. "This!" he said. As they came upon a sharp curve, Ray floored the gas pedal hard.

The Tundra hit the small Ford from behind, propelling the smaller vehicle over the retaining steel barrier. It flew through the air, landing several yards down the steep hillside, and burst into flames.

Ray stopped his vehicle, and he and Scott exited the truck.

As they looked down at the flaming vehicle, he told Scott, "That could have been us."

They climbed back into the truck and proceeded to Palmer, Alaska.

***

Ray's one-level ranch home was equipped with a large, two-car garage, as well as a two-acre horse meadow and barn. As the automatic garage door opened, Ray pulled inside, and the door closed behind them. Inside the garage was another big SUV, a Dodge Ram 1500, four-door crew cab. The vehicle had Nevada plates on it, instead of Alaskan plates, as did Ray's Tundra.

Ray quickly instructed Scott and Nicole to move their bags into the Dodge truck. Then he opened the inside door for them to enter his home. He told the couple to help themselves to hot coffee on the stove but to keep their coats on, as they would be moving out again soon.

Scott and Nicole fixed themselves a cup of coffee each, but Ray was busy gathering a few military-style duffel bags, along with two small assault bags. He went back to his Dodge truck and placed all three in the back cab.

Scott asked him what their next plan was. Ray hurried to his desk and gathered up his laptop computer, along with some books and files. He told them they would be moving out again soon to another location, as the agents were closing in on them now.

Scott looked at Nicole, who told him she was terrified. She mentioned his family back home. Scott was about to question Ray, when Ray shot back, saying that he shouldn't worry; he'd be able to place a call back home once they reached their new location.

Ray went over to the fireplace and fumbled with a few wires under the bricks. He looked at his watch and set a small digital clock. As he placed it back under the fireplace, he smiled to himself and ordered, "Let's go!"

The trio climbed into the Dodge as the garage door opened. Ray pulled out and drove off quickly, the door closing behind them.

"So where are we going to now?" Scott asked.

The truck burned its tires hard into the pavement of the road, and Ray made a hard-right turn onto a small, dirt road that was full of large rocks and mud. "We have to get to another location and fast! There will be agents at my house very soon to kill us, but I made other plans to disappoint them." As he smiled at Scott, they headed through the "Ghost Forest" of Palmer. The trees had died out as a result of the 1964 Great Earthquake.

Ray came to a stop just at the base of Pioneer Peak. He leaned out his window and pressed the button from a small remote beeper. A false door opened inside the peak, and Ray turned on his high beams and drove through. Nicole and Scott were in amazement of all Ray Walker's capabilities. It was as if he had been planning and waiting for this day to come.

***

Minutes later, three large SUVs came to a stop outside of Ray Walker's ranch home. Agent Sean Thomas ordered four of his men to surround the house, as the agent seated next to Thomas pointed an infrared wand at the home that was connected to his headphones. The device would set off a distinct sound if it detected any types of explosives or ammunition within the home.

As the agents covered the front and back doors, the wand emitted a continuous beeping sound. Thomas called to his men on the radio to get away from the house now.

The home exploded outward into a fireball of flames and debris. The four men were blown off the ground and onto their faces from the force of the explosion. Thomas exited his vehicle and just stared at the intense fire that lit up the area, very bright in the dark night. He asked his men if they were all right, and they all responded that they were free of any injuries. He looked at his watch; the time was now 4:00 a.m. He ordered his men to get back into their vehicles and head back to Anchorage.

CHAPTER 5

Ray had food already prepared in a small stove. They were all seated at a small table in his hidden lair. The room within the peak was not big at all—just about 1,300 square feet all around. But it was big enough to store a vehicle inside. Ray was telling Scott and Nicole that he and a friend of his had worked on the construction of the lair for about three years. They had been expecting some big terrorist attack or natural disaster to happen for years. But now the lair was ready to help save their lives, as they fought for the truth.

Scott asked Ray if he could call Kim and Alex and also inform Susan of what was happening. Nicole asked him the same question; she wanted to call her parents in New York, as they would be worried about her, as well as her boss at the paper. Ray told them to relax. He needed to fix a secured cell phone that would block its calls from being tracked by cell towers by removing its tracking strip from within the battery. Nicole asked him how he had come to know all about this and about his interest in UFOs.

"While I was active with the army, I always heard stories of the Roswell case and, of course, Area 51. But you always take it as just rumors and hearsay—until I was assigned to an elite Special Forces squad assigned to retrieve downed alien aircraft from around the world. We were to make sure that whatever we recovered was taken to either Area 51 in Nevada or Wright-Patterson AFB in Ohio. Yes, these secret installations and alien life and technology do exist!" Ray told them.

Scott and Nicole were left with their mouths dropped open in stunned belief as they took in what Ray Walker had just revealed to them.

"The military has small pockets of covert operatives in the army and air force to keep a tight lid on this whole thing. These operatives are charged with ensuring that no one reveals the alien technology and existence to the whole world," Ray admitted.

"I heard of a few rumors when I was in the air force myself—about Roswell, and other famous cases, being hoaxes or misinformation to the public. But now to finally find out that this is all true. I feel it's imperative we break this wide open to the world! Humankind deserves to know the truth about life in other worlds!" Scott yelled.

Ray agreed with him, and Nicole smiled and said she'd be on *60 Minutes* doing exclusive interviews with both Scott and Ray for helping her break the truth about all of these amazing cases.

Ray reminded them that they were all still in grave danger.

Ray handed them the safe cell phone so they could each place a call to their families to inform them of their situations. Then he scanned maps of roads in southern Alaska. He knew they couldn't stay at their location for long—that the rogue agents would find them eventually.

***

In the agency's Anchorage office, Thomas placed a call to his boss, Agent Dorey. He needed instructions on how to proceed.

Dorey was in shock to learn that the couple had found a key person to guide them—someone who had military knowledge of what they knew and skills to match those of his best field agents. "Sean, we need to contain them now. Andrews has a daughter who lives with his ex-wife here in DC. We will need to find and hold them. Andrews will stop this investigation of his in order to reclaim his family from us," Dorey instructed.

"Is that really what you have in mind? Just by holding his family, we can make him and the reporter stop?" Sean asked. He knew Dorey really had other plans for all-out containment.

"Let me seek them out here in DC. You keep tracking down Andrews and his friends in Alaska, and if you have to, end this any way you can, Sean!"

Sean Thomas understood his orders now.

Dorey hung up the phone and looked at the man sitting in front of him—the man who told Dorey what he needed to do next.

***

Susan Morrow entered her office just past 9:00 a.m. Tuesday morning. She turned on her cell phone; a voicemail had been left by someone making a call made from an unknown number at 5:00 a.m. Susan was about to listen to the message when her desk phone rang. She looked at the name on the screen; it was Stephen Clayton calling her.

As she said, "Hello," Stephen abruptly cut her off, telling her to get into his office now.

After he hung up on her, Susan quickly played the message on her cell phone. Scott informed her about what was happening to him and Nicole in Alaska; he said they were being sought by CIA agents and told her to be careful and to look after Kim and Alexandra for him. He didn't know when he would get back to Washington, and she was not to trust Stephen Clayton. Clayton was being informed by the CIA of their motives to expose what had happened.

Susan knew she had no time to call Scott back right then. She left her office to go see Clayton. She was now prepared to face him. As Susan entered his office, Clayton, instructed her to take a seat facing him. He silenced his phone, so he would not receive any incoming calls. Clayton got up from behind his desk and sat on the front end of his desk facing her. She could see the anger in his expression.

"Tell me, Susan. How is it that Scott is back in Anchorage doing his own investigation into what really happened up there on the seventeenth? This entire incident was closed, and only you and I knew what really happened up there. So how does Scott know now? And who is this reporter who is aiding him? And you better not lie to me, Susan!" Clayton very coldly demanded answers from her.

"It's true, Stephen. The reporter is a friend of mine. I admitted to her what really happened that night. And she, in turn, informed Scott of the cover-up bestowed upon us by the CIA!" Susan answered back, anger blazing in her eyes.

Clayton just grinned and rolled his eyes in disbelief.

"Do you have any idea who we are dealing with, Susan? This isn't a game we are playing here!"

Susan shot back that Scott deserved to know what truly happened and that she had felt awful that she couldn't tell him. And she felt that the public had the right to know that our planet was being visited by extraterrestrial life. "Most of all, Stephen, how can you go against your own morals and beliefs as the head chairman of the FAA? You know we are right to share the truth with humanity!" Susan yelled.

Clayton backed off some now and shook his head. "Susan, I'm very sorry. But I was ordered to hold the press conference and make sure this incident ended and went no further than it already has. You and Scott are now on administrative leave as of this moment.

Regardless of Scott's actions now, you have both put yourselves and others in extreme danger. Please go home now and limit your contact with others. I will be in touch as to when you can return to work."

Susan stood up and told Clayton she understood. She left his office to return to hers.

***

Clayton sat back down at his desk. He picked up his phone and placed a local call. "Mr. Dorey, she just left my office. She should be exiting the building through the rear parking lot to get her car. She drives a brand-new, dark blue Volvo S60."

"Good work, Stephen. I will handle it from here on. Just make sure that both Andrews and Susan Morrow left the FAA for professional and personal reasons."

Clayton told Dorey that he understood.

***

Susan quickly returned to her office and thought about what to do next. She gathered her known files of the JAL 1628 case and placed them in her bag. She picked up her cell phone and quickly sent a text message to the number Scott had called her on to let him know what was happening with her.

***

Scott was sleeping, as were Nicole and Ray. When he heard the sound of the phone alerting him of an incoming message, he glanced at the screen.

The message read, "Scott, Clayton has placed us both on leave from the FAA. He was informed by the CIA that you're being helped by others in Alaska, and they want to stop you by any means. What should I do?"

Ray Walker awoke, and Scott filled him in.

Ray looked at his watch. It was 7:00 a.m. in Alaska and 11:00 p.m. back in Washington. Ray instructed Scott to have Susan get out of the building unnoticed and to meet up with Kimberly and Alexandra. He said that all three needed to get out of the DC area as soon as possible—that agents would be coming for them.

Scott quickly sent a text message to Susan.

Moments later, she replied that she understood.

Scott dialed Kim's cell phone; he had to warn her.

***

Kim was just leaving a meeting with fellow staff members when her phone went off. She answered, "Hello."

"Kim, listen to me quick! The CIA is sending agents to hold you and Alex because of my interference in the case I was telling you about. Susan will meet up with you and Alex once you leave work. You have to leave now. Get to Alex as soon as you can! Get some things together for yourselves and get out of DC! Understand?!"

Kim said that she understood. She hung up on Scott and quickly called Alexandra's cell phone to tell her to leave class now and wait for her to pick her up.

***

Susan had waited twenty minutes in her office to give Kim time to get in touch with her daughter and so she could think of a place for them to go and stay hidden for a while. She shut off her cell phone so that no agents could track her location by phone calls. She gathered her purse and shoulder bag, left her office, and headed for the ladies' room, where there was a pay phone.

When Kim answered her cell phone, Susan told her she would take a taxi straight to her house and that Kim would drive them to a friend's location in the outer suburbs. She had no time to return home and get some clothes together for herself. As Kim agreed, Susan slipped out of the ladies' room and took the stairs to the ground floor, so she could exit through the main entrance.

***

Agent Dorey had placed himself and his agents in the rear parking lot. They would intercept Susan when she came for her vehicle. Two dark blue minivans with four agents each waited. In the lead van, Dorey was instructing two female agents; he told them to walk up to Susan casually and kindly persuade her to come with them. He did not want to make a public scene. Only if she refused to go with them would they use force.

In addition, he had two agents posted in the main lobby in case she exited through the main doors.

***

Susan slowly peeked out the first-floor stairwell door. She noticed two men in dark-colored suits who had small two-way radios in hand and knew they were agents sent to get her. She waited a few more minutes, watching as one of the men spoke into his radio.

***

The agents posted in the front lobby had seen no sign of Susan; nor had they heard from Dorey. One of them decided to contact his boss and ask if she had come into sight in the parking lot yet.

"Negative," Dorey radioed back. "One of you go to her office and see if she is there. She must know we're here for her," Dorey instructed.

***

Susan watched one of the men leave and head for the elevator. She knew she had to hurry. Putting up the collar of her jacket to cover her face, she waited for the single agent in the lobby to turn his back to her. Then she slowly exited the stairwell door and passed him unnoticed.

Just outside the main doors, Susan spotted a taxi parked at the curb and passengers exiting the vehicle. She opened the street side door, climbed in, and quickly shut the door. Informing the driver of Kim's address, she sighed as the taxi left the grounds of the FAA facility unscathed.

***

The agent contacted Dorey again to let him know that Susan Morrow was not in her office.

Dorey curses on the radio as he exited his vehicle and marched back into the building. Accompanied by one of his agents, he walked right into Stephen Clayton's office.

"Susan has slipped by us, Stephen. She left her vehicle here, knowing we would be waiting for her. So my question to you is this—where would she go for help?" Dorey screamed at Clayton, who was seated behind his desk.

Clayton thought quietly for a minute. Then he jotted an address on a small piece of paper and handed it to Dorey. "This is Scott's ex-wife's address. I'd bet my money that Susan is going there now."

Dorey looked at the paper and smiled to himself. He radioed his men, instructing them to pull their vans out front. "The time for playing games has come to an end," he said. Then he and his agent ran out of the office to meet the rest of his team.

***

Susan had arrived at Kim's home. She'd instructed Kim to pack lightly for herself and Alexandra. While Kim packed a third bag of items for Susan, Susan took Kim's car keys and went out back, informing Kim and Alex that they would be traveling to a summer home of a friend of hers in the outskirts of Manassas, Virginia, a suburb about thirty-five miles southwest of DC.

As Susan started up the Grand Prix, she noticed three large SUVs pull up around the home. Four agents in dark suits got out of the vehicles, and two went to the front of Kim's townhouse. The two others ran around back and positioned themselves with what looked like Taser guns in their hands. Susan watched, stunned; she didn't know what to do. She sent a text message to Kim's cell phone: "Get out of the house! They're here!"

***

Kim set down a nylon bag and read the message on her phone. Just then, there was a loud knock on the door. A man's voice instructed her to open the door for federal agents. Kim told Alex to remain silent. She slid open the sliding glass window above her bed. The window faced the side of the home and was only a few feet above the ground. Kim told Alex to jump down and get to the car.

Alex did as her mother instructed. Kim pulled out her Glock, as the agents broke through the front door. Kim heard them moving through the living room and up the six steps that led to the bedrooms. She didn't have time to remove the blanks from the pistol and insert the live rounds in the clip that Scott had given her. She knelt down behind her queen bed just as the two men came into view.

***

Alex had made her way to the car, and she and Susan watched the other two agents patiently waiting to enter the back door.

***

Agent Dorey, who remained in the lead vehicle, called on the radio and instructed the other two agents to enter the home now.

***

Kim looked up to see the men come over to the open window and look out. Susan honked the horn to warn her of the additional agents. Kim stood up and fired the pistol; the discharge of the blanks sounded as loud as a real round, and the bright flash blinded the agents. Startled one agent moved to duck and triggered his Taser, shooting the projectiles into the other agent and shocking him full force. The Tasered agent fell to the floor, and Kim shot to her feet, kicking the other agent right in his groin. As the man screamed in pain and fell to the floor, Kim jumped out the window.

Susan darted down the driveway toward her.

Kim jumped in the passenger seat, and Susan floored the gas pedal, shooting right into Dorey's SUV and knocking it into a complete turn. As the SUV hit the side of the home, Susan drove out to the front drive and cruised full speed to the main street. This was their only chance to get away.

***

Agent Dorey looked up from his seat. The front end of his SUV was smashed into the side of the townhouse. He screamed on the radio to his men, instructing them to look for information in the home—anything that would tell them where the women may be going or any leads that could get them Scott or Nicole.

***

While the women drove onto Interstate-95 southbound, Kim laughed out loud as she told Susan and Alexandra how she'd gotten away from those two big men.

Susan explained that they'd be safe at her friend's home for now, and Kim sent a quick text to Scott to let him know what had just happened.

CHAPTER 6

Scott was laughing as he read the text message and told Ray and Nicole that Susan and his family were safe for now.

Ray wasn't that thrilled about the news though. "I'm sorry not to sound so optimistic, Scott, but they are only safe for the time being, as are we for now. Trust me. They will hunt us down and find us. We have to keep moving if we're going to give them the slip."

As Ray continued to look over a land and road map of southern Alaska, Nicole asked him where he planned for them to move to next.

Ray looked up at her and shook his head in confusion. "The smart play is for me to find a clear passage for us. That way, I can get you both to Yakutat, where I have a small plane at the airport. From there, I can get you both out of Alaska and to Montana, where I have friends I trust to make sure we are safe," he replied.

Sensing something else behind his words, Nicole asked what he really wanted to do.

"In all my research here in Alaska, I found that there is a connection with all these UFO sightings in this state and military involvement," he told them. He went over to his laptop and brought up a close-up image of Hooper Bay—a very small city off the coast of the Bering Sea.

"With all the reports of civilian sightings in that area for the last few years, along with the added military presence, I believe there is a secret underground base off the coast of Hooper Bay," he explained. He took out some notes about Hooper Bay and told them about a fire in Hooper Bay in August 2006.

"I remember that fire," Nicole said, thinking of the media coverage at the time. "It destroyed over fifteen acres of land, along with thirty-five buildings and structures, before it was put out. It caused major damage to the city. Officials concluded it was an industrial fire—that it had started at one industrial plant."

"That's what they wanted the public to believe happened. It was either an experimental secret airplane that the air force was testing that crashed or a UFO itself that crashed, right into the heart of the industrial sector of the city," Ray informed them. "The military, along with black ops teams, helped contain and clean up the wreckage of the aircraft. They had it loaded up and carted off by unmarked vehicles, all within an hour of the crash. It was moved to Eielson Air Force Base for a day or two. Then right away, it was transported to Area 51 in order to begin the investigation into what caused the crash and whether it was a UFO. That is what I believe. I believe the military and civilian scientists there planned to break down the craft's propulsion source." Relying on his knowledge as a previous member of the Special Forces containment unit, Ray explained that the scientists wanted to learn how the craft could fly, stops, land and accelerate at massive speeds—up to 10,000 mph!

"I, along with a few other informants, have come to learn that the military has set up several unknown bases for its scientists to work together with some alien races on crossbreeding life forms. By that, I mean that our own government is working with intelligent species of aliens to create a humanoid being that is able to adapt to our planet's environment and exist here."

Listening to Ray's explanation, Nicole began to understand just why these bases and all this information were kept so secret. She questioned him, asking about the location of the bases and why our government was working with the aliens in the first place. She felt that there must be a reason the government would allow any alien race to invade not only our planet but our country as well.

"Nicole, the Roswell case proved to us back then that any alien race has the ability to invade our country's airspace at any time. So with this knowledge, we cooperated with the known peaceful races of aliens—the small grays and the reptilian races, which I know are peaceful beings. On the other hand, there is a race of beings known as the large grays that are violent and want to overthrow our planet and take it for themselves," Ray explained.

Scott erupted in disbelief, demanding to know how Ray knew all this.

Ray told them that it all tied into the secret bases. "The most secretive of these bases is not Area 51 but the Dulce, New Mexico, base under Archuleta Mesa, where, in the summer of 1979, a supposed firefight erupted between the large gray aliens and Special Forces and security personnel in charge of the safety of the scientific staff of the base. It is not known how the large grays were able to gain access to the base. Nor do we know if they were working with the scientists on the biogenic operations and then decided to take over the base."

Both Scott and Nicole were in shock as they listened to Ray Walker's story.

Ray informed them he had learned all of this from a person who was part of the security force at the time this all supposedly happened—a man by the name of Nick Mason. Mason was wounded in the battle but survived and told his best friend of this incident in 1983, right before he passed away from terminal cancer.

Ray told them that Mason had also made schematic diagrams of the base, which was six levels deep. The first four levels were set for security staff checks, along with communications rooms and staff living quarters. The last two levels housed the scientific studies related to crossbreeding human and alien races.

Nicole asked Ray if he knew where these diagrams were and whether he could get his hands on them. The sketches would give them compounding evidence to prove this all to the public.

Ray told her that he had a friend who had received Nick Mason's sketches. "The person who showed me these sketches and photographs of real gray alien beings—which were kept in a cryonic, frozen state—is the same person who received them from Nick Mason. His name is Paul Owens. He is the friend I am trying to get you both to in Montana. He has all the data from the secret bases that are known to us so far recorded.

"The bases are known as either DUMB sites or DUSB sites," Ray continued. He explained that DUMB stood for Deep Underground Military Base and DUSB stood for Deep Underground Submerged Base. A base off the coast of Hooper Bay in the Bering Sea was one of the military's first underwater bases. From there, scientists had been creating a humanoid race. In addition, they were experimenting with flying saucers, along with flying triangle crafts given to them by the grays, in hopes of commanding their advanced speed and stealth performance—for military use only. Ray demanded that they needed to know what was going on at the submerged base in the Bering Sea.

"Ray, listen to what you are telling us," Scott interjected. "You want us to find out what is going on at this base that almost no one knows about. Let's say it does exist. Then what? We get ourselves killed trying to prove this all to the world. Even if your information is wrong and trusting this alien race is not safe, how are we going to get down there, below many miles of ocean, to reach this base?"

Scott continued to plead the case, pointing out that what Walker was suggesting was a suicide mission beyond comprehension.

Walker only yelled back, firm in his conviction. He had no choice. He would proceed with his plans to infiltrate the base and try and stop the grays from completing their real agenda—to take over the planet for themselves. He would do this all on his own, even without Scott's help.

Nicole just looked at Scott. Finally, she nodded her head, yes; they needed to work together with Ray.

Scott and Ray locked gazes. After the two men had stared at one another for a few moments, Scott told him they would help.

Ray smiled. "Thanks," he said, "but we do this all my way. Got it?"

Scott smiled back. "Got it"! he replied.

Scott pondered what had just happened. He knew they were all in a tremendous amount of danger now. But on the other hand, he agreed with Walker; he wanted to get to the bottom of this all now. Scott wanted to discover the truth about all these cover-ups and announce it to the world, with Nicole's help.

"You know what I say, Ray? We head to Yakutat to get your plane. But instead of Montana, we head for Hooper Bay. I want to see this all come out finally! I feel we owe it to the world and all the other good people before us who risked their lives to see the truth come out. Now we are so close to breaking this all wide open. I say, let's go all the way!" Scott angrily shouted out his thoughts on the whole matter.

Ray advised Nicole that she shouldn't get involved with this anymore—that they may not survive the outcome.

"You two macho men might be brave and able to defend yourselves better than I could. But I still want to get to the bottom of this myself! I have been investigating UFO sightings and possible cover-ups for four years now. This is a chance of a lifetime that any journalist would want. I can't let this opportunity pass me by. We will gain so much notoriety, as the three people who proved to the world that aliens exist. I'm going to win the Pulitzer Prize and the Noble Peace Prize with you guys. So let's do it together!" Nicole wanted to aid the men as much as she could.

"Fine," Ray replied. "But we have to be smart, fast and evasive if we are going to pull this all off and have any chance of getting into that base. First, we will head out to Yakutat by 2:00 a.m. We'll have the cover of darkness on our side, and that leaves time for us to prepare ourselves with supplies and much-needed firepower!" Ray smiled as he went over to a military footlocker and opened the lid.

Inside, they saw an assortment of pistols and semiautomatic machine guns, along with a few hand grenades and M18A1 Claymore mines.

Scott looked at Ray Walker, who just flashed him a big grin.

"Let's do it!" Scott said.

The trio shared a smile, and Ray advises them to eat dinner now and to get a lot of sleep because they had a long drive ahead of them, and they needed to move a lot of supplies first onto the truck and then onto the plane.

***

Agent Carlos Dorey had been treated at the local area hospital for wounds received by shards of glass, as the result of the accident while trying to stop Susan and Kimberly Andrews. He was now back in his office in Langley, Virginia. He called Sean Thomas on his cell phone to inform him on what his men were able to find out about Ray Walker.

As Sean Thomas now knew, they were dealing with a highly skilled operative. Thomas admitted to Dorey that he had lost all knowledge of Walker's current whereabouts. The man could be hiding the couple in any part of Alaska.

But Dorey had new information that may lead them to the trio. "Sean, listen to me. We know Walker owns a single-engine Cessna plane. He keeps it at a small airfield in Yakutat. Find them, Sean, and stop them. Ray Walker is very smart, and he has knowledge of what we and the Air Force possess there in Alaska. We can't let this leak to the public." Dorey's tone was fierce, and he was yelling by the time he finished giving Thomas his orders.

Thomas asked Dorey if he had orders to execute Andrews, Walker and the reporter on sight.

"By all means necessary, stop them, Sean!" Dorey ordered.

***

It was just passed 10:00 p.m. and Susan was making sure all the windows and doors to the two-story log home were secured.

Kimberly had fixed dinner, and the women sat down to enjoy the meal and talk about what they would have to do next.

"I locked all the doors and windows, and I pulled out the phone lines from the phones, so no one would be able to call us here," Susan informed Kim.

Kim replied that she'd thrown all their cell phones out the window of the car so they couldn't be traced by cell towers. Also, she and Alexandra had parked the Grand Prix out back and covered it with branches and brush.

Susan noted that, even with the safety precautions they'd taken, they couldn't stay here for long. The CIA would eventually find them.

Alexandra started to cry. She didn't yet know what this was all about or whether she would ever see her father again. Susan explained the whole situation to her and admitted that their lives were in danger.

"Well, as far as protection goes, I have two clips of live ammunition that Scott gave me," Kim told Susan. "But that this isn't much for protection against them."

"I searched around the house, and I was able to find two flashlights, along with a flare gun with two shells. My friends who own the cabin are not hunters. So we are lacking survival equipment. But the good news is, we have lots of food stored in the meat freezer in the basement, along with canned goods."

"How will you be able to contact your husband and family, Susan?" Alexandra asked.

Susan laughed. "My ex-husband and I don't talk anymore," she explained. "But as for my parents and my sister, I'll have to find a way to let them know that I'm fine and that I no longer work with the FAA."

Alexandra suggested that Susan send them an e-mail. She had her laptop in her book bag with her.

"That's great!" Susan replied. "We can also send an e-mail to Scott. He can read his e-mails from his cell phone."

Alex ran and retrieved her laptop, set it up on the table, and turned it on. Susan instructed Alex to tell Scott that they were together and fine for now but that they couldn't tell him their location, as it seemed much safer if he didn't know for now. Alex also typed that they hoped he and Nicole were fine and that they'd all be able to see each other soon. Alex finished typing the e-mail and sent it to Scott. Then the trio settled in to wait for his response and instructions on what to do next.

***

Just after 2:00 a.m., Ray had Scott and Nicole load supplies and food into his Dodge truck. When Scott told him they were all ready to go, Ray placed his footlocker of weapons in the back passenger seat next to Nicole. He handed Scott a loaded .45 caliber pistol with two extra full clips. Scott put the shoulder holster around his left shoulder, and Ray did the same with his own .45 pistol.

The hidden door opened, and Ray drove out of his secret lair, as the door closed behind them. Ray warned the couple that they had a long drive ahead of them. He would stop to rest and let Scott drive the last two hours of the four-hour trip to Yakutat.

Scott took out his BlackBerry phone. He checked his e-mail account and opened the one Alexandra had sent him. He read it aloud to Scott and Nicole, letting them know that the women were safe for now. Scott replied to Alex's e-mail, telling her that he and Nicole were okay for now, as they were traveling to another part of Alaska. He suggested that the women find another location soon to move to. He knew they couldn't stay safe wherever they were for long.

From behind, Nicole gently touched Scott's shoulder. She asked if he was really worried about his family.

"I'm really worried about them, yes. I wonder if what we are doing now is really the right plan." Scott second-guessed himself about their plan to uncover the truth.

Ray told him that he, too, was concerned for Scott's family's safety, but they had no choice now. They had to unlock the key to one of the biggest secrets of all time.

"Scott, don't worry. I'm sure your family and Susan will be fine. We will be back home soon enough with the most shocking story ever broken to the public!" Nicole agreed, trying to raise Scott's spirits.

He held her hand and told her that he hoped so.

Ray glances over at them. He didn't say what he was thinking—he knew that they would either succeed or die trying to uncover the whole truth about what was going on in Alaska.

***

Acting on his orders from Agent Carlos Dorey, Sean Thomas dispatched six of his men to Yakutat Airport. The men were to intercept Scott and his companions. Agent Dorey believed that Ray Walker had knowledge of the secret of the military's Deep Underground Submerged Base under the Bering Sea. By all means, now he would have to kill the trio.

***

It was just after 4:00 a.m. and Ray and Nicole were getting some sleep as Scott drove through the port city of Ketchikan. They would board an Alaska Marine Highway ferry in order to cross the Inside Passage waterway to reach Yakutat. There was no highway system in the coastal panhandle region of Alaska due to the high mountains and rough passages.

Scott nudged Ray to let him know they were about to board the ferry. As Scott paid the toll clerk and gently drove through the raised gate arm, Ray noticed a big SUV with dark, tinted windows pull up next to the tollbooth. He thought to himself for a moment, unable to shake the feeling that something wasn't right here. The ferry master instructed Scott to drive to the end of the rear of the ship and park the truck in the right space. Ray noticed the ferry master guiding the large SUV two spaces to the left of their vehicle.

Nicole awoke and looked around at where they were. Noticing the serious look on Ray's face, she asked him what was wrong.

"Nothing," he said as the ship's horn sounded, alerting the crew and passengers that they were ready to cast off.

Scott also noticed that Ray was uptight and kept looking over at the SUV across from them. He too asked Ray what he was concerned about.

"Scott, when we reach a good distance from the shoreline, we are going to be attacked by the men in that vehicle," Ray alerted him.

Both Scott and Nicole were stunned. Ray went over a plan of action with them.

***

The ferry had reached the middle of the passageway. Now, only a half hour remained of the ride to Yakutat.

Two men dressed in black slowly emerged from the SUV's rear passenger doors. Two others emerged from the front doors. They moved in pairs to the front and rear of Ray's truck. In an instant, they rushed the vehicle. But to their amazement, they found no one inside. They stood still for a moment with their pistols in their hands.

From behind, Ray raised his large tantō knife. The blade sliced into the first man's neck from behind, and shot out the front of his throat, causing blood to gush from the open wound. Ray then raised his .45 pistol in his left hand and shot the men to his left, both in the head.

Scott emerged from under the Dodge and shot the last two attackers each in the head, killing both instantly.

Ray instructed Scott to help him place the bodies back in the vehicle in their seats. Then he told Nicole that all was clear. She emerged from the Dodge, as she had hidden on the floor.

Ray pulled out one of the men's identification cards from his wallet. As he examined the name on the dead man's CIA card, he pointed out that these men had been sent to kill them.

Nicole crossed her arms around her shoulders. She started to cry, knowing that she could have been killed. Scott went over and hugged her, trying to comfort her.

"It was either them or us," Ray said, as they returned to the Dodge.

Ray informed them that the agents had waited for the right time to attack—when the crew of the ship was relaxed and not paying attention, and the sounds of the ship's engines and the waves would drown out the sounds of the gunshots. As daylight, was breaking through the clouds, they came upon the docks of Yakutat. The foghorn sounded from the ferry, alerting everyone that they were about to dock.

Ray returned to the driver's seat. As they were cleared to drive off the ship, Scott asked how much farther it was to the airfield. Ray answered that they were only another half hour away.

Nicole kept a small journal with her. She wrote down everything that was happening to them. She told the men that the journal was to help her write her exclusive exposé for her paper.

CHAPTER 7

The sheriff of Yakutat, along with two of his deputies, responded to the ferry. The ship's captain and ferry master had come upon the bodies of four men in their vehicle.

Sean Thomas dispatched two men to the scene, instructing them to explain to the local sheriff that his men had been killed in an attempt to apprehend three dangerous fugitives. He gave no names of the three people they were searching for. He spoke with the sheriff by phone, instructing him that his agents would track down the fugitives on their own. They didn't want any assistance from Alaskan law enforcement. The sheriff was only to inform them if the fugitive's vehicle turned up somewhere in the state. The sheriff agreed to Agent Thomas's instructions.

***

Thomas called his boss to inform Agent Dorey of what was happening now. They needed to find a lead—to anticipate when and how Scott Andrews was contacting his family.

"Sean, let them get to Ray Walker's plane in Yakutat," Dorey instructed. "Once they take off, I will have them followed by helicopter to see where they are heading to. My guess is that they're heading to Hooper Bay. We need to stop them before they find the critical information they seek. As far as Andrew's family and Susan Morrow, all we need is another e-mail to Scott from his family, and we will pinpoint their location!"

"I understand, boss. I will let my men know that they should follow Scott and the others closely but be very stealthy so as not to expose ourselves to them again," Thomas replied. He knew that his boss was taking orders from high above—orders to stop Andrews and his friends and family.

***

At 7:20 a.m., Ray and Scott had finished loading all the supplies into the single-engine Cessna. Ray parked his truck in a large storage shed behind one of the hangars. By 7:45 a.m., Ray was cleared for take-off from Yakutat Airport. His flight plan was set for Hooper Bay, due to land by noon Alaskan time.

Scott told Nicole that they were making good time. He quickly sent an e-mail to his daughter to let her know that he and his companions were traveling to Hooper Bay—another destination that was part of their investigation.

***

Moments later, Alexandra received the e-mail from Scott. Her mother and Susan read the short sentence.

"Wow, Scott must have really gathered a lot of information up there," Kimberly said. "I hope he and his friends are safe. We don't know what to expect from these people."

"We have to think about moving ourselves," Susan reminded them. "We can't stay here much longer, and we can only check into hotels with cash, as they can track our credit card transactions. And we are short on cash."

Alexandra searched online for cheap motels.

***

At his desk, Carlos Dorey was on the phone with Sean Thomas, who'd just called to let Dorey know that Ray Walker had taken off from Yakutat.

A call came in on Dorey's other line. He put Thomas on hold.

"Carlos, we just traced an e-mail sent from Scott Andrews to his daughter. The women's location is in Manassas, Virginia!" the caller reported.

"Find their exact location and move agents to intercept them," Dorey ordered.

He reconnected with Thomas on the other line, informing Thomas that he'd closed in on Andrew's family here. He instructed Thomas to reach out to the military in Hooper Bay—to let them decide how to handle Andrews and his friends.

Dorey hung up on Thomas and ran to the control room to be briefed on the location in Virginia.

***

The women and Alexandra were gathering their things to leave the small house. They planned to travel to a motel in the city of Arlington, Virginia. They went in and out of the house, placing items in their car. As their attentions were distracted, two dark-colored minivans approached the home very slowly, one from the front and one from the back of the house. Both vehicles contained three agents each. The vehicles came to a stop, as the lead agent gave instructions by radio. He instructed his men in the front to cover the vehicle so the women couldn't escape and informed the two agents he was with to enter the house through the back door.

One of the men took out a short, metal crowbar. He stuck it in between the door and its frame and, with all his strength, forced the frame free, wedging the door loose. The agents fixed their pistols with silencers, but Dorey had given them orders to take the women alive.

Three agents entered the house. Two of the men moved from room to room as the third moved straight from the back to the front of the house. When he encountered Susan, who had a small travel bag in her hands, she screamed for Kimberly to run now. Susan threw the heavy leather bag at the agent. He moved to avoid the impact and quickly fired two rounds from his pistol, hitting Susan in the back. She fell forward to the floor.

Kim heard Susan scream in pain. She grabbed her daughter's hand and ran out the front door toward their car. They were met by the other two agents, who pointed their pistols right at them. Kimberly shielded Alexandra behind her. The lead agent instructed them in a firm voice to remain where they were. Kim knew she had to comply with their orders. The other agent came over and instructed them to get into the backseat of the minivan. He led them into the van and secured the doors behind them.

The agent who shot Susan came out the front door and told his boss that Morrow was dead. The lead agent cursed at the agent loudly, telling him to secure her body, clean up the house, and instruct one agent to drive the women's vehicle and get rid of it. Then he returned to his van, instructing his driver to take them to Langley, Virginia.

While they were driving toward the turnpike, Carlos Dorey called the cell phone of his lead man. He explained that they had Scott Andrew's family, but accidentally killed Susan Morrow while trying to apprehend her. Dorey cursed at him loudly over the phone, stating that Morrow was vital to finding Andrews and his friends in Alaska. Dorey said he would deal with his men later and instructed the agent to bring Kimberly and her daughter to CIA headquarters, hanging up the phone before the agent could respond.

***

In the backseat, Kim was holding her daughter. Alexandra was crying, not knowing what was going to happen to them. Kim whispered to Alexandra that everything was going to be all right.

As they drove on, Kim became angry, not only because these men had killed Susan, but also for what they were putting her family through. "You bastards!" she yelled defiantly. "You killed Susan! You have terrorized my daughter and me, and you tried to kill Scott! For what? To cover up some UFO sighting!"

The men just looked at one another as their captive yelled. When Kim stopped shouting, the lead man turned around and met her eyes. "My dear Miss Andrews, you have no idea what Scott got himself involved with," he responded coolly. "All he needed to do was accept the official cause of the incident that everyone agreed on, and this whole thing could have been avoided. But now we have to deal with the problem he has created, and we'll have to use ulterior methods, thanks to him and his reporter friend."

The agent's eyes narrowed, and he yelled as he continued, "The lead agent in charge of the case will meet with you once we get to Langley. My advice for you and your daughter's sakes is to cooperate with us fully!" With that, he turned and faced forward again.

Kim knew she was helpless to defend herself and Alex. So for now, she would listen and do what the agents told her.

***

Scott checked the time on his watch. It was just past 1:30 p.m. Alaskan time. Scott commented to Nicole and Ray that it had been over an hour since he'd received a text message or e-mail from his daughter. He was now worried about his family and Susan.

Ray told them that they were just over the small city of Chevak. He Ray radioed the airport in Hooper Bay to confirm his altitude of 14,000 feet and to confirm their landing at 14:20 hours. The control tower responded that they were cleared to land.

***

Sean Thomas was flying in an OH-58C black helicopter, which was trailing the small Cessna plane. He was aware of what had transpired with Andrew's family, who were now in the hands of the CIA. He was awaiting orders as to what to do when they landed in Hooper Bay. He instructed the pilot to stay a good distance behind the plane. He didn't want to give themselves up, and he knew that their helicopter was much faster than the small, single-engine Cessna. They could catch up to Walker at any time.

Just then, Thomas received a radio transmission from their field office in Alaska instructing him to force the plane to land by any means possible. He was to take the passengers alive. Thomas acknowledged the orders. He quickly radioed for two more helicopters to join them. Thomas instructed the snipers to be prepared to fire in the plane but not to harm the pilot and passengers. The shooters were to cause structural damage that would force the plane to crash land. Then his agents would be able to apprehend Andrews and his friends.

The two helicopters, which were positioned just outside of Hooper Bay, raced into the air in order to intercept the plane before it landed at its destination. Thomas shouted his orders to his teams. The sharpshooters in both helicopters readied their M82 .50 caliber rifles. The pilots made a complete 180-degree turn around the Cessna and now trailed behind Thomas's lead helicopter in a triangle formation pattern. Thomas motioned to the pilots to close in on the plane on either side and to first try to reason with them to land. Both helicopters raced ahead to catch up to the small plane.

Both Nicole and Scott yelled to Ray as they watched the two helicopters flank the plane on either side. Ray made an angry face and cursed. He yelled instructions, telling Scott and Nicole to hurry and brace themselves and fasten their seatbelts. Ray looked to his right side as he heard one of the pilots instruct him to land the plane at once. Ray smiled at the crew in the helicopter to his left as he flipped them off with his middle finger. They all watched on, as the sharpshooters took aim with their rifles. Thomas ordered them to open fire.

Ray knew his plane couldn't outrun the helicopters, so he steered the plane hard to the left. Simultaneously, the shooters opened fire at the Cessna. The shooter on the right was able to get a clear hit on the plane's fuselage as it banked to the left. The .50 caliber rounds caused a big hole in the plane's fuselage. The fuel began to seep rapidly from the opening.

Ray banked the plane hard toward the helicopter at his nine o'clock bearing. The crew was stunned, but their sniper shot his rounds, hitting the windshield and left side window. As the glass shattered, shards hit Ray in the face. He screamed in anger.

His left wing clipped the helicopter's tail rotor. The blades shredded the flaps off. At the same time, the rotor snapped off its shaft. The helicopter spiraled out of control and plummeted toward the earth at high speed, bursting into flames when it hit the ground, instantly killing all on board.

Scott screamed to Walker, asking for directions as to whether they should hurry and equip their parachutes.

Ray screamed back, "No." They weren't high enough. He was losing control of the plane and would have to land hard. He told Nicole and Scott to brace themselves. He was able to level out the plane but went into a sharp dive in order to get away from the other helicopters.

**

Thomas yelled over the radio to the remaining team, "Follow the plane's smoke trail." He ordered all of his team members to get ready to engage Walker on the ground. However, he wanted Andrews and the woman taken alive.

**

The plane descended rapidly at a steep angle. It was now less than two thousand feet above the earth. Ray fastened his seatbelt tightly. He was able to maneuver clear of the high mountains and glimpse a patch of dense forest below. He told Nicole and Scott that he would try to land in the forest, as it would give them cover.

Soon, the plane was just above the thick treetops. Ray gingerly dived into the thick forest as the tree branches scraped and broke off the bottom of the plane. He glimpsed a patch of a clearing coming up and shouted to his passengers to brace for a hard impact. The aircraft took a thunderous hit from a large, thick tree as it ripped the right wing in half. The windshield and side windows exploded inwards as thick branches broke the glass.

Finally, the plane broke free of the thick brush, and Ray steered, guiding the plane to its left. The remaining left wing hit the ground hard, causing it to bounce off the ground and snapping its landing gear off. Ray again glided hard to the ground, and the small Cessna skidded along the grass and dirt. Ray looked up and spotted another patch of thick trees up ahead. He let go of the wheel and screamed at Scott and Nicole to keep their heads down.

The plane smashed into the large, thick trees at full force. The crew of three was thrown back into their seats very hard, as the plane finally came to a stop.

After a few moments, Scott was able to regain his senses. He looked up and saw smoke coming from the cockpit. He reached over and touched Nicole's arm, asking her if she was all right. Nicole responded that her left arm was hurting her and she was shaken up. Scott then yelled for Ray, asking how he was.

Ray very slowly reached up with his right hand and pulled himself up in his seat. Blood covered his right hand and flowed down the right side of his face. Ray ignored the pain in his body; he knew the plane's engine was on fire and fuel was leaking from below.

"Scott, get Nicole out of the plane now!" Ray shouted. He leaned to his right side and, with a strong kick, opened his left side door. He jumped out to the wet, muddy ground.

After getting Nicole a good distance away from the plane, Scott returned to Ray and the plane. Ray ordered him to hurry and get the duffel bags with the supplies. Scott took out the two heavy bags. Ray looked into the two large crates that contained the explosives and ammo. He knew they couldn't carry the heavy boxes, so he emptied a large military assault bag and placed the two Claymore mines in the bag, along with several hand grenades and boxes of ammo.

Scott returned to Nicole, who was taking shelter under a few trees and bushes. He removed a first aid kit and started to tend to her wounded shoulder. He looked up when he heard the sounds of helicopters coming toward their location. "Ray! Hurry; they're coming!" Scott yelled.

Ray loaded a flare gun then ran toward Scott and Nicole and cover.

"What are you doing?" Scott asked.

Ray, who was fixing the two wires into the blasting caps of the Claymore, just looked at him. He and Scott looked up as the surrounding tree branches and dirt began to swirl around them. The two black helicopters landed only twenty-five yards away from them, next to the crashed plane.

Ray slammed the Claymore into the ground on its legs. He whispers to Scott and Nicole that they needed to move back very silently now. Scott slung one of the duffel bags over his shoulder and helped Nicole to her feet. Ray fixed the other bag over his shoulder and carried the assault pack in his hand. Trailing the detonator wire on the ground, he pointed to Scott to head to a cover of large rocks behind them.

***

Sean Thomas ordered his men to surround the plane. Very carefully, the agents closed in on the plane. One agent looked through the plane's window and motioned back to Thomas and the others that the plane was empty.

"Spread out and find them," Thomas yelled, as he exited his helicopter with pistol in hand.

His men begin to look at the ground and search the area for signs that would tell them what direction the trio had taken.

***

Ray armed the wire into the plastic detonator. He took out his Desert Eagle pistol from the duffel bag and placed it in his side holster. The flare gun sat next to him. "Now I'm pissed off!" he whispered. He waited for the right moment.

***

The agents armed their rifles, preparing to fire. Thomas reminded them that he wanted Andrews and the girl taken alive, as he gave the order to eliminate Ray Walker, noting that the latter was very dangerous to handle.

One of the men noticed a blood trail leading away from the plane toward a set of trees behind the plane. He motioned with his right hand to the others, signaling that they should head in that direction. Five men very slowly moved toward the trees, while Thomas remained with the other three by the helicopters.

***

Ray waited patiently, but in an aggressive mode, as the agents got closer to the Claymore.

With rage in his eyes, Ray pressed the trigger. It set off a thunderous explosion, and the flames and shrapnel from the mine found their marks on the exposed agents.

Thomas and the remaining agents hit the ground for cover.

Ray stood up and fired the flare gun at the wrecked plane. It hit the leaking fuel, igniting a fire.

Thomas yelled to his men to move now, as the plane exploded into a ball of fire, blinding the men at once.

Ray emerged from the trees, opening fire with the Desert Eagle. One round caught an agent in the head. Dead, the man flew off his feet. Ray quickly aimed again and fired at one of the helicopters through the windshield. The rounds struck the pilot in the neck and head. As he slumped down on the controls, the helicopter lifted off the ground several feet into the air. It then reversed and came crashing back down to the ground, exploding on impact.

Ray quickly changed magazines and started firing at the other two agents, who had barely made it to their feet. The rounds hit them square in the chest, and each fell to the ground dead.

Before Thomas could even aim his pistol at Walker, Andrews kicked the gun right out of his hand. Meanwhile, Walker pointed his weapon straight at the pilot of the remaining helicopter. He ordered the pilot to leave the engine on and him to exit the craft.

The pilot did as he was ordered. Ray instructed Scott to load their bags and equipment into the helicopter and hop aboard, keeping Thomas and the other man covered with his pistol. Scott threw the duffel bags in, and he and Nicole climbed into the helicopter.

Ray turned his attention to Thomas. They stared one another down. Ray held his gun in his left hand, as he made a fist with his right hand and swung, hitting Thomas in the face hard. As blood shot from Thomas's mouth, he again met Ray's gaze. "You three will not uncover what you seek!" he shouted. "You're not as good as you think you are, Mr. Walker!"

Ray just smiled back at him and said, "We will just have to wait and see about that, Mr. Thomas!"

Scott yelled to Ray to hurry so they could leave.

Ray kept his gun fixed on Thomas and the pilot as he walked backward to the helicopter and climbed in. Sitting in the pilot's seat, he took hold of the controls and lifted off.

***

Thomas kept his eyes fixed on the helicopter until it was very high in the air. Then he took out his cell phone. He needed to get in touch with his superiors and set their plans for Hooper Bay.

***

As they were flying, Scott retrieved the first aid kit. He tended to Ray's injured right hand, which was bleeding heavily. Scott quickly cleaned the gash with iodine and covered it with a clean dressing.

Scott then turned his attention to Nicole, who had a laceration on her lower left arm; her left shoulder was also deeply bruised. Scott cleaned and dressed the cut. He gave them both Motrin for the pain, telling Ray that was too close.

Ray just kept his eyes straight ahead, as he followed the navigations to Hooper Bay. He knew the agents would either try to intercept them again midflight or wait till they reached Hooper Bay. "Look, Scott, we need to prepare ourselves now before we reach Hooper Bay. They will no doubt want to kill us on sight, even before we land."

Scott just shook his head in disbelief. He didn't know what they could do to save themselves from another attack. "Well, even if we make it there in one piece, do you have a plan as to what we are supposed to do there? How are we going to find out about this base in the Bering Sea? Are we supposed to dive down there or take a submarine ride down to see if this place actually exists?" Scott yelled.

Nicole also questioned Ray's motives.

Ray turned and smiled at Scott. "I have a plan," he said, with fire in his voice. "Trust me!"

CHAPTER 8

Thomas was able to reach his contacts in Hooper Bay and let them know to expect Walker and his companions late this evening. He also ensured that Agent Dorey was made aware of what happened in Alaska.

***

Dorey made his way with his men to their isolated location just outside of the DC area, where they were holding Kimberly Andrews and her daughter. Dorey requested to speak to Kim alone. He would try and convince her to help him get Scott to stop what he had planned—to stop trying to discover the truth behind the JAL 1628 case and the whole UFO cover-up in general. Before it was too late, Dorey had to try and contain the situation, without any more lives lost.

He entered the small room, leaving Alexandra in the living room of the large house with two female agents to watch over her. Dorey closed the door behind him and sat at the table facing Kim. He placed a large pile of documents on the table, then introduced himself to Kim. She remained silent, unimpressed by his title and that he was with the CIA. He went over, starting from the beginning, how Scott had come to be involved in the case, bringing up to the current point now.

Kim thought back to what they had done to Susan and how they had forced her and Alex to be on the run and in fear for their lives. She couldn't contain her anger with Dorey and his people. "Mr. Dorey, is it?" she shouted. "I am grateful up to now, that your people have treated my daughter and me well. However, what I don't like and what is inexcusable is that your agents murdered my close friend, Susan Morrow, for no reason at all! And you've scared my daughter to death for no reason at all!"

"Miss Andrews, I am not at liberty to discuss with you in full detail what this is all about. But this much I will admit to you— there are many things that governments of the world can't share with the public, for reasons of not only a country's national security but to keep all life on Earth safe from harm."

A military veteran, Kimberly Andrews was sharp and intelligent enough to know of what Carlos Dorey was talking about. "So what do you want me to do for you?" she asked in a low, soft voice. "I only want one thing from you and the CIA. Please release my daughter and me unharmed, and you have my word I will not leak any of this information to anyone."

Dorey just smiled at her. He insisted that he wanted to release them. But first, he needed her cooperation on something very important. "I need you to convince Scott to stop this suicide mission of his with that reporter, and the very dangerous person whom he thinks is aiding him. I will need you to come to Alaska with my team and help me convince Scott that what he got himself involved in here is very dangerous and that the truth can't be told to the world just yet. You have my word that he and his friends will not be harmed! And you will all be united again and released."

But Kim knew he wasn't telling her everything. "I know there is something more you want from him. What is it, Mr. Dorey?"

"I know that Scott is in possession of certain voice tapes, video and documents that I want from him. If I have all these items back from him and I have his word that he will give up his plan to prove what he thinks he knows to the world, I will make certain that he and his friends will be unharmed and allowed to return to their normal lives. Now, isn't that what you want for your daughter and for Scott?" Dorey asked her.

For a moment, Kimberly simply stared into his eyes. Then she said very softly, "Yes."

Dorey broke into a smile as he told her that she was doing the right thing for herself and her family. He picked up the desk phone and placed a call to the Alaskan office. Then he told Kimberly to get ready, as they had a very long journey ahead of them.

Kim hoped that, by agreeing to work with the CIA, she could save not only Alexandra and herself but Scott as well.

***

It was early evening and daylight faded in the seaport town of Hooper Bay, Alaska. Ray landed the helicopter in a remote field about two miles away from the heart of town. He insisted they needed to find shelter and rest for the night, as it was now early November and the nights were getting colder.

The trio carefully walked through town until they found a convenience store that was still open. They purchased food and supplies. Scott paid with cash, knowing not to use any credit cards, which would have given the authorities and CIA agents a means of tracking their location.

As they left the store, the time was now just after 10:00 p.m. Ray led them down to the industrial area where the fire of 2006 had taken place. They found a building that was still under construction to use as shelter for the night. Ray lit the area with a small battery operated lantern, and they spread out on the cool surface.

"Okay, Ray, we made it to Hooper Bay. I see from the amount of construction still going on here that this fire was massive," Nicole said, as Ray and Scott laid out some of the supplies for use.

Ray took out a few maps and notes for himself, lighting a glow stick to read them better.

"So how are we going to get below the freezing waters of the Bering Sea to this supposed base, which I think is a crazy idea of yours?" Scott asked, giving Ray a look that said, *You might be able to fly planes and helicopters and defend yourself very well, but what you intend to do is beyond the normal realm of any person.* "But the bigger question is, how are we going to get out there, to begin with?" he added. "Do you plan on stealing a boat?"

Ray looked up at Scott and answered, "Well, first, we *are* going to steal a boat! And then we will use the same means of transport that the military and scientists are using to get down there—from the supposed offshore oil platform that is directly over the base. It's their key way of hiding their work there." Ray showed them the schematic diagrams of the oil platform, about fifteen miles off the Alaskan coastline in the Bering Sea.

"So once we commandeer a boat to get us out there, what then?" Nicole asked. "Do you think the three of us will be any match for them at all?"

"First, it will be me and Scott only, Nicole. This is far too dangerous for you to be involved with, so you're going to stay here on shore while Scott and I infiltrate the platform," Ray instructed, as he took out the remaining Claymore mine and a few hand grenades, along with their remaining firearms and ammunition. Ray added that he would find a way for them to be able to compromise security and gain access to the platform.

"Look, you two stay here until early morning," he said. "I'll be back before first light. I need to find some other needed supplies and the boat for us." He placed the weapons and his diagrams back in the duffel bag. Ray then gave Scott a loaded pistol with extra magazines. As he got up, he holstered his pistol in his right side holster.

"Nicole, I'm just curious. Are you married or do you have a significant other, if I may ask?" Ray asked, smiling at Nicole.

Confused, she made a face and said, "No. Why do you ask, Ray?"

Ray smiled and said, "This is why!" He grabbed her around the waist, pulled her tightly into his chest, and kissed her deeply.

At first, Nicole was shocked by his action, but soon she relaxed and kissed Ray back just as deeply.

Scott looks on, stunned.

Nicole and Ray gently broke off their long kiss. She smiled at him and touched his face. "Ray, please be careful."

"I will. I promise I will be back before daybreak with a boat and a few other supplies. Now, I suggest staying off the phones so they will not be able to trace our locations."

Scott and Nicole both acknowledged his orders. Ray armed two of his pistols and holstered them then set off in the darkness toward the docks of Hooper Bay.

Scott told Nicole to get some sleep, while he did a weapons count. He wanted to see how many firearms and explosives they had left. He counted three more .45 caliber pistols. Ray had one .45 with him, along with the Desert Eagle with twelve fully loaded magazines, four hand grenades, and the last Claymore mine. Scott just hoped this was enough for what Ray had in mind to get past the security points.

Scott sat back down and took out his cell phone. He scrolled through his text messages, wondering why he hadn't received one from Alexandra since yesterday. He was worried about her and Kimberly. Scott knew what Ray had said about phone contact. However, he was nervous, and he told himself that he just had to know how his family was doing. He sent an e-mail message to Alexandra.

***

Aboard a large, white Cessna Citation X jet plane, Carlos Dorey, along with eight other agents and the flight crew, were bound for Hooper Bay. Both Kimberly and Alexandra were in tow. Dorey assured Kim that no one would be hurt and this would all work out for everyone—provided Scott and his friends gave themselves up. An agent came over to Dorey and whispered in his ear. Kimberly could only guess as to what it was about.

Taking in the information—that Alexandra had just received an incoming e-mail—Dorey nodded. The agents had been anticipating this. Dorey listened to the identification number, showing that the e-mail was sent from Hooper Bay, Alaska.

He whispered back, "Trace the exact location that the e-mail was sent from and then get Thomas to move in on them."

The agent understood his instructions and went back into the cockpit of the plane. Dorey looked at his watch and told Kim they would be arriving in Alaska by early morning, so she and Alex should get some rest now. Then he stood and headed for the cockpit, ready to learn what was happening in Hooper Bay.

***

Ray scanned the boat dock and the many boats secured by their lines to the dock. He needed to scope out the dock before he made any sudden move on any of the boats. He knew he had to get a high-speed jet boat that would get him and Scott out to the site fast.

He spotted a relatively new boat, docked in the third space to his left. As he watched, a lone security guard walked back and forth on the dock. Until the guard passed, Ray remained hidden behind a wall of stacked small boats. The guard went into the small security office and closed the door. Ray quickly took out his large survival knife and jumped into a fairly new, twenty-foot Sea-Doo jet boat. He cuts the three ropes that secured it to the dock. He then used the knife to wedge open the steering column and wedge out the ignition. He placed it back in as if a key had been used to start the boat. As the engine turned on, Ray shifted the boat forward and pulled out into the bay. He looked back as the guard made his way to where the boat was docked.

Ray hit the throttle, speeding up and heading toward a point near where he'd left his friends. Once there, he opened the boat's rear seat to check the cargo box. He saw a few items that would come in handy. He smiled to himself and headed down the shipping lanes.

***

Nicole was sound asleep. Earlier, Ray had given his jacket to her to use as a pillow on the cold surface. Scott was sitting with his back against the wall, pistol in hand, keeping watch. It had been nearly an hour since Ray set out to find a boat and Scott was now drifting in and out of sleep. He awoke to a faint sound in the distance, and then he felt a sharp, cold blade under his chin as he opened his eyes. One man in black held the knife to his throat, as three other men stood guard over them. Scott didn't even say a word as his gun was taken from him. One of the men motioned for him to stand up, and Scott complied with the order.

Another man in black bent down to Nicole, who was still asleep. He covered her mouth with his gloved hand. Her eyes snapped open in shock as he whispered to her to remain silent and get up. She looked up at Scott. He nodded, indicating that she should do as the men asked. Nicole slowly got up and was gently pushed next to Scott. The four men now surrounded them. Two of them kept their weapons fixed on the pair, as the other two scanned the area, anticipating Walker's return.

Sean Thomas emerged from the dark SUV and walked up to them. He stared at Scott and Nicole, a cold mean look on his face.

"You know, Miss Martone, your involvement here has caused us plenty of time and effort to keep all this quiet. It was you who brought Mr. Andrews into this situation, which should have ended the day after it happened!" Thomas shouted. As he yelled out his anger for the trouble the pair had caused his department, he told them of what had happened to Susan Morrow and that Scott's family was in their custody.

Nicole broke out crying upon hearing that her good friend, Susan, had been killed. Scott cursed at Thomas and demanded that his family be released. Scott hugged Nicole to comfort her and she cried into his chest.

***

From behind the parked SUV, Ray Walker observed what was going on. A moment later, he spotted the oncoming headlights of another vehicle approaching very quickly. Ray laid down under the SUV to hide as the car came to a screeching halt. Three men in suits exited the vehicle and joined Thomas and the others.

"Scott, you're very interested to know what's beneath the oil platform! And you want to see your family," Thomas yelled. "You're about to see both right now!"

Two of the men pulled him away from Nicole and led him to their car. Nicole yelled out to Scott, but the other agents held her back. Helplessly, she watched as Scott was driven away from her.

Thomas then turned his attention back to Nicole. "Now, Nicole, as for your involvement in this matter—we need for you to give us all the information that both Susan Morrow and Thom Brown supplied you and Mr. Walker with. We need the copies of the pilot tapes, along with the printout of the plane's flight plan!" Thomas ordered, a cold stare in his eyes.

Nicole, angry now with what Thomas was demanding of her, stared back at him defiantly. She smiled. "Well, you can kiss my Italian ass! No way am I going to give up that information to you!" she screamed.

"It's great that you have that attitude, young lady, because we have ways of changing your mind without hurting you, my dear!" Thomas yelled. He instructed his men to take Nicole over to their vehicle.

***

Staying low to the ground, Ray crawled out from under the SUV and took shelter behind a concrete barrier. He knew he had to act now to save Nicole.

***

Thomas told Nicole that he had received orders to bring her back to their location in Anchorage. But before they went back, he needed to tell his superiors that they had recovered the voice tapes and documents that were in Ray Walker's possession.

Still defiant, Nicole would not talk or in any way reveal where they'd left the items behind. The agents forced her into the SUV. Thomas climbed into the backseat from one side, and one of his men climbed in the other side so that Nicole was seated between them.

***

Ray looked up to see what was going on. He looked at the three men surrounding the vehicle with their semiautomatic rifles in hand and armed his Desert Eagle.

***

Thomas pulled off Nicole's jacket and pushed her pink sweater up her left arm, as his agent readied a hypodermic needle attached to a syringe. The syringe was filled with sodium pentothal, which in addition to being used as an anesthetic, was also effective, in a low dosage, as a truth serum.

Nicole tried to break free from Thomas's grip, but he held her left arm firm as he ordered his man to give her the injection.

"We will see how cooperative you are now, my dear!"

As the needle was about to pierce her skin, a round was fired through the left side window. It struck the agent in his left temple, his blood splattered Nicole's and Thomas's faces, as the agent fell dead.

A steel anchor, thrown through the air, struck another agent in the head, and he fell to the ground.

Ray jumped to his feet, firing his gun. The rounds struck two more agents in the chest, and they flew back from the tremendous force of the Desert Eagle's rounds.

Thomas, keeping his head down, took out his pistol. He grabbed Nicole's hand and told her to be still and exit the vehicle.

Slowly, she came out of the door first. Thomas followed her out and yelled to Walker not to shoot, "Or I'll kill your friend." He held his gun to Nicole's head and held her around the waist using her as a shield to confront Walker.

Angry, Walker lowered his weapon to his side as he walked closer to them. He passed the fallen agent whom he had hit with the anchor. The man was trying to get up. Ray shot him in the head without remorse. He moved closer to confront Thomas.

"That's it, Walker! Any closer and I will kill the girl! Try me!" Thomas yelled.

Walker stared into his eyes, showing nothing but hate for Thomas.

"You're a dead man, whether you hurt her or not, Sean!" Walker screamed in defiance. "I will stop you people!"

Walker raised his gun slowly; Thomas knew he had to kill Walker now. Quickly, he aimed his gun at his assailant, who jumped to his left side, as Thomas fired at him.

The rounds missed Walker and he flipped his body forward. He fired off a round, and the round found its mark, striking Thomas dead center in his head. Thomas flew backward and fell to the ground, dead.

Nicole fell to the ground to avoid the gunshots. She slowly looked up as Walker looked around to make sure the agents were dead. He told her it was all clear now. She got up and ran to him, and they embraced one another and kissed.

"Ray, are you crazy! You could have gotten killed!" she yelled at him, crying, and they kissed again.

"Don't worry. It's all right now. You're safe, Nicole," he told her.

She told him that the other agents had taken Scott away to the oil platform, and Ray replied that he knew. "I have to get out there to save him. But I can't go right now; they'll be expecting me."

Nicole asked how he would be able to get out there unnoticed by the surveillance cameras and armed guards.

Ray looked at Thomas's body and smiled to himself. "I have a plan, but first, I want to make sure you're safe. Then I will offer them a trade—our information for Scott's release," Ray told her.

"What?! After all we did to get this information, you're just going to give it up to them? They will kill you and Scott no matter what, Ray!" Nicole yelled.

Smiling, Ray told her to trust him, that everything would be fine. He went over to Thomas's body, hauled it up off the ground, and placed it in the backseat of the SUV. He then told Nicole to get in. He collected two of the AR-15 rifles, along with their extra 30-round magazines, and placed them in the backseat along with Thomas's body. Ray jumped in the driver's seat, and they sped away.

CHAPTER 9

Scott was taken aboard a black helicopter. As the bird approached the platform, sunlight was just breaking. It was almost 7:00 a.m. From its outward appearance, the platform was a typical working oil rig that was occupied by oil workers and tankers. But as the helicopter landed on the platform, Scott observed many surveillance cameras posted on all decks of the rig. He also spotted men in dark coveralls with rifles slung over their shoulders.

The helicopter landed on the platform. Four armed agents, along with a head man wearing a fine, dark blue suit and raincoat, were waiting. Scott was escorted off the helicopter and handcuffed.

The head agent in charge stepped forward to confront Scott. "Welcome, Mr. Andrews. My men will see to it that you are made more comfortable in your own quarters for now. Then we will need to have a very long discussion about some recent events that you are involved in," said Agent Carlos Dorey.

Dorey's men led Scott to a set of elevator doors. The doors opened, and the group stepped into the car. At first, it appeared that the inside walls of the elevator were a dark color. But as the car started to descend, the walls became a transparent glass panel. Scott looked out into the blue ocean, shocked, as the facility led into a working underwater base. Large lights were fixed to the structure to illuminate each of the ocean levels. The base extended all the way to the floor of the Bering Sea.

The car stopped halfway down the clear elevator towers. Dorey's men escorted Scott out into a huge and brightly lit hallway. They came upon another armed guard standing outside an open room. Scott was pushed into the room and Dorey followed in with two men. The room was small; it had a bed, bathroom and a desk in the corner. Dorey instructed Scott to sit on the bed, and Scott complied with the order. One of the men removed his handcuffs from his wrists.

"Scott, I will have food brought to you, and then I think you should get some rest. I don't have much time here, as we need to go over many things that impact our national security." Dorey smiled then walked past his men, who followed him out and locked the door behind them.

Scott looked around the small, windowless room, wondering if the agents were going to kill him.

***

Ray drove to where he had docked the jet boat. He stored the needed supplies on the boat, along with Thomas's body, then had Nicole take shelter in a nearby abandoned storage shed. He placed the remainder of their bags in the shed and told Nicole to get some sleep, saying that he would be back very soon with food for them.

Ray drove to a strip mall that was about a mile and a half away, parked the SUV and made sure he left no items behind in the vehicle. He spotted a two-door, newer model Monte Carlo and was able to use a slim Jim to open the driver's side door. He climbed into the vehicle and used his large survival knife to pry open the steering column's ignition switch, as he had done with the boat.

Ray placed it back inside the column, as the car started. He quickly drove out of the mall and went to find food for Nicole and himself.

***

It was nearly 2:00 p.m. Nicole was sound asleep when a hand gently stroked her face. She opened her eyes to see Ray smiling at her. She smiled back and sat up, and they gently kissed one another. He told her that he had food and hot coffee. She started to eat, as Ray went through his assault pack bag and took out his laptop computer and some blank CDs. He pulled a slim, portable CD burner from the bag.

Watching him, Nicole asked what he was doing.

"Give me your copies of the pilot's voice tapes and the radar transmissions showing both the plane and the UFOs together," he told her.

Nicole retrieved her tote bag and took out the discs for Ray. She watched as he plugged the portable burner into his laptop and inserted the main disc into the laptop and a blank disc into the burner. Seeing the stack of five blank discs, she gave Ray a puzzled look. "Why are you making so many copies?" she asked.

Ray looked at her. "Because I'm going to take the original copies with me when I infiltrate the platform. My best bet is that, if I have what they want, they will trade the discs for Scott. If not, they'll kill us anyway," he answered.

"Ray, this is crazy! You alone are no match for God-knows-how-many armed guards they have in that place. Do you really expect them to let you just drive the boat up to the platform and climb aboard?"

As Ray listened, he inserted another blank disc into the burner. "Yes!" he answered. "First I have a plan to make it there unnoticed. Then I will let them know I'm there to talk to them. My old friend and former colonel in charge of my unit, Mike Sharpe, is in charge of the base now and will be more than happy to see me again. He taught me, along with the other members of our containment unit, all we had to know in order to contain downed UFOs all over the world and about the different alien life forms. He taught us how to protect ourselves if their bodies contained any known viruses that would be harmful to us. And he taught us to eliminate any civilian witnesses that would get in the way. He is a very smart man and almost a hero in the army. But I found him to be very coldhearted; he has no remorse for taking human life if someone gets in his way."

Nicole looked worried. She was afraid that Ray was going to get himself killed fighting to prove to the world the truth about alien life forms.

He finished making all the copies of the discs, took the originals and gave Nicole three copies, telling her to secure them away in one of her bags. He went to the car and retrieved some items he'd recently picked up. On the floor of the shed, he combined regular household cleaning agents in a small plastic tub.

Nicole watched him mixing the products together, and she knew what he was doing. "You're making a bomb?" she said simply.

"Yes. I'm using ordinary household cleaning products that contain glycerin and sulfuric acids to create nitroglycerine," he instructed, squeezing toothpaste from a tube and mixing it into the concoction. He explains that an ingredient in regular toothpaste—propylene glycol—when added to any nitrate could become a deadly combination. He mixed the ingredients together with a plastic spoon, then used his knife to cut off the tips of each glow stick and poured out their fluids. He instructed Nicole to hold one stick while he poured the highly powerful liquid chemical explosive into each stick. He then cut off four long pieces from a candlewick spool and sealed them into each stick with duct tape leaving a piece of the wick sticking out.

"Wow! Who taught you all this cool stuff?" Nicole asked.

Ray told her that he'd learned most of this from his Special Forces training and that most of the explosives and hand-to-hand combat training he and his platoon had received had come from Colonel Sharpe.

He took out two clear waterproof bags about four inches long each. He placed a book of matches and approximately two inches of wick into one bag and sealed it up then poured some of the chemical into the other bag and sealed it. He took off his shoes and placed each bag into his socks, hoping that, if he got caught, this would provide a means of escape.

"Look, right now they must be interrogating Scott about the discs in our possession and where we are hiding," Ray told Nicole as he looked at his watch. It was just after 3:00 p.m. "I'm running out of time now. You take the car and get back to the small town of Chevak. Be very careful and stay on the main roads. When you have to stop and get gas and food, pay by cash only so they can't track you by credit card purchases." As he offered this advice, he gathered all his needed equipment together to take with him on the boat. He then loaded the remaining items in the Monte Carlo.

"Ray, you are heading out on this mission now with hardly any sleep and energy left. How do you expect to get into that place before they riddle your body with bullets?!" Nicole demanded.

"For starters," he grinned, "I drank four of these already." He opened another Red Bull energy drink and downed it quickly. Then he made sure his pistols were fully loaded and holstered on both sides. Next, he made certain that both his AR-15s were fully loaded. He slung one over his shoulder then smiled at Nicole.

"You be very careful Ray and find Scott for us."

"I will. Once you get to Chevak, check into the Moose End Lodge on the outskirts of town. Ask for the manager Billy Eagle. He will take care of you until I meet you there soon. Do you understand?"

Nicole nodded and hugged him tightly. Once again, they shared a passionate kiss.

"I promise, you're going to have the biggest story of all time," he told her, touching her face softly. Then he picked up his assault pack and headed to the boat.

When he was out of sight, Nicole got into the car and drove to the main highway that led out of Hooper Bay.

***

For two hours Agent Dorey had been sitting down talking with Scott. He wanted to know where Ray Walker was and why he hadn't heard from his top agent, Sean Thomas, since this morning.

Scott answered that all he remembered was that Dorey and the other agent had found him and Nicole and that he had been taken away and brought here.

"Well, Mr. Andrews, let me bring you up to speed on what has been happening the last few hours. My agent, Sean Thomas, is missing and the bodies of his men have been recovered at the same location where we found you and Nicole Martone, who is also missing. So did Nicole kill my men? I don't believe so. I think it was none other than your other friend, Mr. Walker, who singlehandedly accomplished this incredible act."

Scott just smiled feeling relieved that Ray had saved Nicole. "If you want me to tell you where they might be, I don't know. I do know that it seems that you and your people have pissed Ray Walker off! And I want to know how my family is! They have nothing to do with this at all, and I want to know how they are doing."

"I will be honest with you, Scott. Your ex-wife and daughter are here in Alaska safe and sound. I am seeing to it that they are being treated very well and no harm will come to them. But what I need most from you is two things only. First, I need all the copies of the voice tapes and radar scan from flight 1628 that night. Then, before I can unite you with your family, I need your word that you will forget about this whole incident as well as all the information you have learned from Ray Walker, as he is a very dangerous man. Then I will see to it that you are still employed in your top position with the FAA."

As Dorey explained what he wanted, Scott thought about his options. He wanted to make sure his family was safe, but he didn't want to give Dorey and his agents the satisfaction of knowing they'd completed their mission to cover up this case. "Like I told you before, I don't know where either Ray or Nicole kept the discs. You will have to find Nicole or Mr. Walker and ask them yourself. As far as this incident goes, I promise you I will not say a word to the media about anything I have learned. I just want to be united with my family. Prove to me that they are all right!" he demanded.

Dorey smiled before taking his cell phone from his jacket pocket and placing a call. He instructed the agent on the other line to put Miss Andrews on the phone. Then he handed his cell phone to Scott.

"Scott! Where are you? Are you all right?" Kimberly's voice showed she was very upset.

"I'm fine. How is Alexandra?" Scott asked.

Kimberly told him that she and Alex were well and being held at some undisclosed location. She asked again where he was.

But before Scott could answer her, Dorey told him not to discuss where he was or what was happening. Scott nodded in agreement.

"Look, Kim, I'm sorry for all that has happened, but be assured that you and Alex will be taken care of. And I will see you both soon. I promise you," he told her as the line went dead.

Angry, he looked up at Dorey.

"I'm sorry, Scott. I couldn't keep that line open for very long. You see, I gave you my word that your ex-wife and daughter will be taken care of. I know you got involved in this case unwillingly, as the information was brought to your attention by both the reporter and Miss Morrow. I'm sorry about what happened to her."

Scott replied that he didn't believe him.

Just then, there was a knock on the door. An agent whispered for Dorey to come outside for a moment. Dorey excused himself telling Scott he would be right back.

"Sir, it looks like Agent Thomas is approaching in a ski boat. He didn't make any attempt to contact us. Should I send out a patrol to intercept him?" he asked.

Dorey asked the agent if Thomas was with anyone else. The agent told him that Thomas was alone and wearing dark sunglasses.

"Let him dock at the east side and then notify me once he is cleared to come up. I want to meet with him right away!"

The agent said he understood his orders.

Dorey returned to Scott's room and informed him he would return shortly and let him know how much longer it would be before he was united with his family.

***

Just under ten miles away from the oil platform, the Sea-Doo jet boat roared through the very choppy waters of the Bering Sea. Ray hid under a white, vinyl tarp, just next to the passenger seat. He was still able to look up and see how far away he was from the platform. Ray had affixed Thomas's body in an upright position at the wheel of the boat, placed dark sunglasses over his eyes, and tied his wrists to the wheel. Ray knew this was the only way he could get close enough to the platform and then ditch into the water before being seen.

Ray looked up again very slowly from under the tarp. He saw a beacon strobe light on the east side of the platform signaling the boat to dock there. Ray slowed the throttle some and gently steered the boat to the east, then slowed to just 5 mph. He gripped the assault pack in his left hand as the boat passed right under the platform. He quickly grabbed hold of the rope with which he had tied himself to the left rail and leaped into the water. He was pulled by the force of the boat as it slowly moved into the dock.

The armed guards yelled at Thomas to stop. The boat hit the dock and came to a stop with the engine still running. One guard jumped onto the boat, while four others surrounded the boat with their weapons drawn.

The guard on the boat shut the engine off. He looked at Thomas and saw that the agent was held in place at the wheel. Just as he yelled to the others, informing them that Agent Thomas was dead, a burning glow stick landed next to him in the boat. It detonated into a fireball, and the docked boat exploded killing the five guards instantly.

Ray searched his pack. He placed the loaded magazines in his pockets along with two hand grenades, leaving one AR-15 rifle and the Claymore mine in the assault pack, which he hid in a storage cabinet on the dock. Ray armed his rifle as the elevator doors opened and three more guards come out.

The guards looked at the devastating fire. One of the men grabbed a fire extinguisher and doused the flames. The other two looked around at the bodies and wondered what had caused the explosion.

Ray came out from behind the pillar and smacked one of the men in the back of the head with his rifle. He opened fire on the other two as they turned around. The rounds from the AR-15 cut the guards down. Ray took out his survival knife and slashed the throat of the guard on the floor.

A warning siren blasted throughout the platform. Ray knew he had to head down below in order to find Scott and whatever was really going on at the lower levels. He stepped into the elevator as the doors closed, saw that there were six levels below and two upper levels for the platform. He pressed the button for the fourth level, determining that he'd start there and work his way down.

***

As the warning siren sounded throughout the facility, Colonel Mike Sharpe, the commander in charge of the base, headed into the communications room on the third level. There, video screens showed the feeds from surveillance cameras that monitored the entire compound. Sharpe orders one guard to zoom in on the fire at the dock, and they watched a host of guards working to put out the fire.

Captain Chris Harris, who was in charge of security, radioed Sharpe to inform him that eight men were dead as a result of the explosion and gunfire. Sharpe ordered the monitor's technician to play back the video that had captured the dock just before the explosion took place. He watched the boat come into the dock, and then something was thrown from below, causing the explosion. As the intruder's body came into view, Sharpe ordered the tech to pause the tape and zoom in on the man's face.

Sharpe was stunned as he recognized the man. "Well, well. Ray Walker! You're still alive after all these years," Sharpe whispered to himself. He radioed back to Harris, instructing him to have his men sweep each level in teams of four. He added that they had a very dangerous intruder who was intent on inflicting serious damage to the compound.

Harris told Sharpe he understood. Then he ordered three men to come with him and radioed to his men to begin the search of all levels.

"Captain Harris, I want the intruder alive!" Sharpe yelled over the radio. "Do whatever you must to contain him, but he must be taken alive!"

Harris confirmed his orders.

"What are you up to Ray?" Sharpe said to himself. "I look forward to meeting you after all this time."

Sharpe talked to Carlos Dorey by phone, informing him that Walker was the cause of the explosion and that Walker was now searching the levels for proof of what was really going on. Dorey, who had complete authority over Sharpe and his men, ordered him to contain Walker any way he could.

Meanwhile, Harris had his men sweep each level, intent on finding and containing the intruder.

***

Ray stepped out of the elevator and peered behind the corner. He spotted a group of guards running down the hallway away from him, and he ran in the opposite direction. Ray noticed the surveillance cameras along the hallways, but couldn't worry about whether they saw him. He had to find out what was going on and try and document it as quickly as he could, and he had to get Scott out of there if he could find him.

***

Sharpe spotted Walker on the monitor as his old friend ran by a camera. "Son of a bitch! He's on level four!" he shouted out loud.

He picked up his radio and yelled to Harris, telling him to get five teams down to level four to contain Walker.

Harris acknowledged Sharpe's orders and screamed to his men to follow him now.

***

Ray came upon two thick, metal doors that required an access key to open them. He knew he couldn't stop, even though he was very curious to know what was behind those doors. He ran back around the left corner and waited for a moment as the door opened slowly outward; two guards came out and looked around the area for Ray. They spotted him on their camera inside the wing, as they walked past the corner.

Ray moved in swiftly behind them. With his leg, he swept the guard on his left side, knocking him to the floor. He kicked the guard on his right in the stomach. As the guard fell, Ray grabbed his head and snapped it backward breaking his windpipe and let him drop to the floor dead. Ray pulled out his long knife and thrust it down into the first guard's neck with all his might, killing the guard instantly. Ray got up, holstered his survival knife and darted through the open doors just before they closed.

He raced down the dark corridor, passing a security desk checkpoint and reached another bank of thick metal doors, which were locked. Like the other doors, only a security card key would open them. Ray didn't hesitate; he took the butt of his rifle and smashed the card reader off so he could work on the exposed wires. He crossed two wires of different colors together and the door unlocked. Ray pushed it open and ran forward, his rifle drawn. He made his way to a large glass window and peered inside. He was shocked by what he was seeing with his own eyes.

A naked, male human body floated inside a large tank of fluid, which was joined by pumps and oxygen tubes to another tank. The second tank contained a large gray alien who, like the human, had tubes and lines coming out of its body. Ray noticed two men in long white lab coats who appeared to be scientists standing over a computer and specimen jars. The men raised their hands to surrender.

Angrily, Ray raised his gun and shot. In a burst of gunfire, rounds destroyed the tanks' glass and punctured both life forms. The scientists yelled for him to stop shooting as they hit the floor to take cover. From behind one of the tanks, smoke began to rise. Then the tank exploded in a ball of fire causing the other tank to explode simultaneously.

Ray hit the floor, just as guards came running through the doors. Ray stayed low. He pulled the pin from a grenade and hurled it at the approaching guards then rose to his feet and ran while dodging the guard's rounds. He leaped through a glass window to his right side just as the grenade exploded amongst the four men.

Glass and debris shot over Ray's head. He looked to his left and noticed another set of tanks. Both life forms were clearly set up for some kind of human bioengineering experiments. Seeing more guards coming at him, he ejected and put in a fully loaded magazine. He lay face up on his back and opened fire. A bullet pierced one of the guards right in his neck. Ray took aim again and hit another man in his legs. The man fell to the floor screaming in pain.

As Ray reloaded, a loud voice yelled his name out, ordering him to stop shooting. Ray heard the footsteps of many guards running toward him in different directions, ready to box him in. From the floor, Ray looked up and to his left; a host of armed guards were coming at him from that direction. Other guards were carefully looking into the rooms through the shattered window, trying to pinpoint his location. Ray knew he would either be killed now or taken alive. He pulled the pin on his last grenade and hurled it out the shattered window. He quickly took out his last three explosive-laced glow sticks and hid them in a bottom drawer of the desk he was hiding under.

The grenade exploded, and he shielded his face from the blast and flying debris. He heard the voices of many men screaming in pain.

As he moved out from under the desk, guards on both sides of him pointed their rifles at him. Still on his back, Ray aimed at them in return.

Again the voice instructed him to stop. "That's enough, Ray! Lay down your weapon now, and we will not harm him!" the voice ordered.

The smoke and flying debris had cleared somewhat in the room. Ray looked up to see Scott with his hands cuffed behind his back, an official in charge of the men holding a pistol to his head. The man with the gun demanded that Ray give up now. Ray cursed out loud, but he knew he had no choice. He told the man that he'd comply.

As soon as he threw his rifle to the floor, the guards moved in on him. As the other guards covered him with their weapons, two men picked Ray up and a third hit him in the gut and again in the back of his head. They stood him up straight.

Captain Harris ordered his men to check Walker thoroughly, as they removed both his Desert Eagle and Glock pistols, along with all his extra magazines in his pockets and his long survival knife. Harris ordered the guards to remove Walker's jacket and shirt, as well as his combat boots. The two guards checked his feet but didn't remove his sock. Ray stood perfectly still, as he was placed in steel handcuffs. One guard yelled to Harris that the subject was secured. Harris holstered his weapon and told his men to take Andrews back to his location. Harris then called on the radio to let Sharpe know they had Ray Walker secured.

"Good work, Harris. Take him up to level one and keep six men on him at all times. I will meet you there momentarily!" Sharpe ordered.

Harris instructed his men to move Walker up to the security control level.

CHAPTER 10

Ray had received cuts to his hands and face when he'd crashed through the lab's large window. Harris had ordered the medical staff to treat Walker and give him some medication for the pain. Ray was now sitting in a room with steel walls and a heavy steel door without any windows. The only thing the room was equipped with was a steel bed frame, a sink, and a toilet—the same type you would find at any modern prison. Ray was seated in a chair with his hands cuffed behind him. His shoes were removed, as were his socks. But the guards had never looked under his feet as they'd taken his socks off. Ray was cautious not to raise his feet up. He just kept them flat on the cold floor. He had affixed the waterproof bags with DUO surgical glue to the bottoms of his feet to make sure they would stick to his bare skin well. Two armed guards were posted outside the room, and two more armed men were in the room with Ray.

As Ray could hear talking coming from outside, he knew the ones in charge were going to confront him now.

***

Agent Dorey was speaking with Sharpe and Harris before they entered the room.

"These are the three copies of the disc that were recovered from his inside jacket pocket. They are copies of the voice recordings and radar from flight 1628 when it encountered the UFOs," Sharpe informed Dorey.

Dorey took the copies from Sharpe and simply stared at the discs for a while. He contemplated how he would confront Walker with the hard evidence that was now in their possession. Dorey instructed Harris and Sharpe that he wanted to ask Walker if he knew Nicole Martone's whereabouts and if he had any other copies of the discs or any other evidence regarding UFO or alien technology that he could leak to the public.

The three men entered the room, and Ray and Colonel Sharpe locked eyes. Pure hatred shown in both men's eyes.

"Sergeant First Class Ray Walker. How nice to see you again after all these years," Sharpe said. "We meet again under very tedious circumstances. You made a hell of a welcome for yourself here!"

Ray laughed at his captors and said that he wasn't able to get his hands on a daisy cutter bomb.

"Your skills haven't changed one bit, Ray. You took out fifteen men and injured seven others. And you caused millions in damage to our facility and the very important cryogenic labs we have on level four," Sharpe told him.

Ray smiled and said that Sharpe had taught him all he knew.

"Well, Mr. Walker," Dorey interjected, "we did find the three sets of discs in your jacket's cargo pocket. It looks like the original along with two copies. So my question to you is, where are the other copies you made? And where is that very pretty reporter?"

"You have all the copies I made right there in your hands. As to where Nicole may have gone, I have no idea. We went our separate ways when we reached Hooper Bay, and your people picked up Scott Andrews. So maybe you can ask your point man, Sean Thomas, where she might be," Ray answered, a smile still on his face.

"Don't be a smart ass, Ray! You know you killed Thomas and his men!" Sharpe yelled.

Ray asked what their plans were for Scott Andrews, who was only a civilian with many friends at the FAA. He pointed out that there would be an inquiry if Scott turned up missing, along with his family.

Dorey told Ray not to worry about Scott Andrews—that he would take care of him.

The three men talked in a circle, whispering so that Ray was unable to hear the conversation. Ray looked around the room; the door was his only point of escape, as he was, after all, in a holding cell.

***

Dorey was instructing Mike Sharpe that he would have agents look for Nicole in Hooper Bay and the other surrounding cities. He noted that she couldn't have gotten far in only a few hours. Sharpe insisted that he would try and get more information from Ray and have him terminated when the time was right.

Approving Sharpe's decision, Dorey left the room and headed to the communications room, leaving Sharpe and Harris alone with Walker.

***

"I'm warning you all right now—if you harm that girl, I will kill you all!" Ray yelled at Sharpe and Harris.

Harris started to laugh, and Sharpe asked Ray if Nicole was now his girlfriend.

"Maybe she is," Ray replied.

"You know, Ray, you were one of the best operatives on our containment team. For six years, you did what you were ordered to do—locate and contain any life forms that were deemed a threat to our planet's existence. But you seem to have developed a soft spot for alien races, which are violent towards humans," Sharpe said.

"That's what you and the supposed leaders of your group are saying. I only knew of one race of aliens that seemed to be a threat to us and other forms of life on other planets. So if I'm wrong and you're right, tell me what you're doing at this top secret base all the way up here in Alaska and what really happened at the Dulce, New Mexico, base in 1979 under Archuleta Mesa? Tell me about the supposed super-secret base we have that is even more classified than Area 51," Ray demanded.

Sharpe moved closer to Ray, pure hatred in his eyes. "Ray, when you were a part of my team, you were told only what *we* wanted you to know. But since you're not going to leave here alive, I will tell you all that *you* really want to know."

Ray couldn't believe Colonel Sharpe was going to admit everything about the alien agenda to him.

"First of all, Ray, we learned way before the Roswell Incident of 1947 of aliens invading our planet. In 1909, a company of cavalry soldiers chased a group of bandits in the desert of Truth or Consequences, New Mexico. They followed the bandits into a secluded cave and came upon large, triangle-shaped UFOs and small alien beings. That was our first encounter with aliens in New Mexico. During World War II, their crafts paced our planes and kept a close eye on us as we made war. They were so curious to know of our technology, of how we made the H-bomb at White Sands. That curiosity led to the Roswell crash, and we were very fortunate to get our hands on that craft and those beings. It taught our scientists to duplicate their propulsion system, which led to many of our modern planes and spacecraft for NASA."

Ray couldn't believe what he was hearing; he tried to think of a way to make it out alive and tell all of this to Nicole. They would shock the world when they exposed this news.

Sharpe continued to explain, mentioning many other cases that Ray had never even heard of before. "Roswell wasn't the only crashed spacecraft we were able to get our hands on. In 1953 outside of Kingman, Arizona, we came across another crashed saucer that was very small. There were only two small beings on board. So, you ask, what does this have to do with the Dulce Base? What of the continued visitations of the smaller gray aliens and the large gray beings? We started to build the Dulce Base in 1979, under Archuleta Mesa. It was going to be our second top secret base, after Area 51. When our scientists and geologists were excavating an unknown cavern about four miles deep under the mountain, we discovered that the large gray aliens had already set up their own colony there—one that had been established for over hundreds of years. The security force engaged the aliens as they were attacking our scientists, which led to a horrific firefight, causing a total of sixty-six to seventy-two deaths."

The details Sharpe was admitting to Ray were amazing. Ray had heard rumors of the supposed fight at the Dulce base, but now he was learning it was all true.

"So you see, Ray, the large grays have been here for God knows how long, waiting to take over our planet. New Mexico was the prime area for them to study our military might and weapons. So now, ever since 1979, the Dulce Base has been our stronghold from which to fight them.

"The smaller grays come from a planet in the Zeta Reticuli star system, almost thirty-nine light years away from our planet.

Their planet is under constant attack by the large grays. So they came to Earth and made contact with us to warn us of the threats of the large grays to both our worlds and to share our technology with them."

Sharpe stopped, as if concluding his speech, but Ray knew there was something more the colonel wasn't telling him. "If all you're saying is true, then what is the need for this base way up here? And what about the program for crossbreeding humans with the large grays? Unless the same black ops team you work for has an agenda of its own—to make a super soldier, able to adapt in all climates, and not only those of our world but worlds beyond, and able to fight like no human being can! So you are also working with the large grays, taking advantage of their superior strength and size. Wow, talk about stabbing your friends in the back!" Ray yelled.

In response, Sharpe and Harris just laughed.

"You know, Walker, you're a smart son of a bitch! Too bad you didn't see things our way and the size of our paychecks!" Sharpe turned to Harris and ordered him to have Walker placed under tight guard until they had Scott Andrews removed from the base. Sharpe told Ray that he would be eliminated once his friend, Scott Andrews, had returned to the mainland.

With that, he and Captain Harris left the room.

Ray thought about what do to next. He was still seated in the chair with his hands cuffed behind his back and knew he would be unable to break free of the cuffs. But he also knew he still might be able to use his hands to set off the explosive. He decided to wait awhile, as Sharpe and Harris had just left the room. He wanted the guards to be relaxed before he made his move.

***

Sharpe returned to his office where Carlos Dorey was waiting for him. They needed to discuss what to do with Scott Andrews; what Ray Walker had said about him was right. They would be asking for more trouble if they decided to eliminate Andrews, a high-ranking FAA official.

"Mike, we have to release him with the presumption that he will not talk to the media about this. I feel it was the reporter and his assistant that pushed Andrews to look into this case, but we eliminated Susan Morrow, so that issue is gone."

"What about the reporter? We have to stop her before she can write anything or conduct an interview for television," Sharpe replied.

"Even if we let her make it back to Washington, DC, we could let her write anything she wants. We have total deniability on this subject, and we still have enough time to pull the plug on her if she does manage to get people in the media to listen to her."

Dorey and Sharpe both agreed on a plan that would try and contain the situation without any more loss of life. Sharpe made a call to his security staff instructing them to bring Scott Andrews to his office.

***

As nightfall was coming on, Nicole made the hour drive back east to the small town of Chevak. Not too familiar with the town and the roads, she asked for directions when she stopped and filled up for gas at a local gas station. The friendly attendant directed her to keep traveling along the same major road to the end of the fork at the light. Then she was to make a sharp left, and the Moose End Lodge would be on the left side. Nicole thanked him and hurried back to the car, driving quickly along the road.

Nicole wondered how Ray knew all these people in such a big state like Alaska. Thinking of Ray and Scott, she prayed that they were still alive and well. She saw the brightly lit sign to the lodge and pulled into the front parking space. She looked around as she got out of the car and went inside the office.

As she entered, she heard voices coming from a television in the back room. She looked around the sign-in desk and rang the bell for help. A tall, native Alaskan man came through the open door. He stood about six foot two. He had long, black hair that was showing grays on the sides, which he kept tied back in a ponytail. He put his glasses on to see better and smiled at Nicole as he greeted her. "How may I help you, young lady? Do you need a room?" he asked.

Nicole returned his smiles. "Yes, I would like a room," she replied. "And are you Mr. Billy Eagle?"

Handing her a pen so she could sign her name in the guest ledger book, he looked up at her and said that he was Mr. Eagle.

"I'm a friend of Ray Walker; he told me you could help me?" Nicole said.

The smile left Billy Eagle's face and turned into a very serious look. He closed the ledger book, not wanting Nicole to sign her name. He came around from behind the desk and looked out the window. "Is that your car parked out front?"

Nicole told him that it was.

"Wait for me in the back lounge," Bill instructed. "I will move your car for you."

In the lounge, Nicole looked out the window. She watched Billy drive the car to the back of the motel, where a garage door opened automatically. He drove in and the door closed behind him. A moment later, Billy came out of a side door and returned to the motel. He entered the lounge, bringing Nicole's bags with him, and told her to have a seat. Then stated that she would not be staying in a guest room but in a room in the back of the motel. That way he could keep a close eye on her. He asked if she thought she had been followed on her way to Chevak. Nicole told him she didn't think so, but Billy made a face and then went over to the wall where he had two shotguns displayed. He picked one up and pumped it to chamber a round. Then took a box of shells out of a drawer and sat back down on the couch facing Nicole. He told her she would be safe here for the time being then asked her how she had come to know Ray Walker.

Nicole told him all about the JAL 1628 flight and how she and Scott had gotten involved. She also told him about what was going on at the oil platform and Scott being held captive.

Billy was shocked to learn all this; he was surprised that Ray had gone through with his promise to find out what was going on here in Alaska and break this whole UFO secrecy wide open. "Ray advised me he was going to find out what was going on at the platform in the Bering Sea, ever since I told him about the UFO crash here in Chevak four years ago."

Nicole asked him if he'd seen it happen.

Billy simply nodded yes. "I saw the UFO fall out of the sky and crash into the heart of the city." Billy went on to tell her that was how he'd been introduced to Ray Walker, former military operative and investigator of UFO cases. He said that, when the UFO had hit the large fuel tankers, it had started a massive explosion and fire in the industrial sector of the town. The military had arrived within minutes of the crash to put out most of the fire, but mostly to retrieve the UFO and get it to the platform as quickly as possible— before the media or civilians could ask any questions. He said that he'd believed that the military had to have known the craft was in distress or that it had already been in military possession, perhaps in some kind of a test flight, when it crashed.

"Well Billy, I'm not sure what Scott Andrews's fate is as of now. But I do know that Ray plans to not only rescue Scott but also to find out what is going on at that place and destroy it if he can."

"My lord, he is going to get himself killed!" Billy yelled. He tried to decide what he should do.

Nicole showed him the discs that she and Ray made of the cockpit voice recordings and the radar video of the UFOs. Billy took them from her and smiled.

"What are we going to do?" she asked.

"First, I'm closing the lodge for a while; I just went on a sudden vacation for myself. We have to make a quick stop at a friend's home of mine. I need some equipment, and he has to do something important for us real fast. And then we are heading to Hooper Bay!" Billy replied.

Nicole agreed. She wanted to make sure that Ray and Scott were all right.

Billy got his Toyota Sequoia and Nicole climbed into the passenger seat. The pair drove off into the dark Alaskan night.

***

Ray was growing impatient. He'd waited in the room for four hours now. He'd been released from the chair for a few moments so he could eat a tray of food and use the toilet. But Colonel Sharpe had ordered that he be cuffed again right away.

Ray knew his best chance to escape would be late into the night when there would be fewer guards roving the hallways.

***

Carlos Dorey and Colonel Sharpe met with Scott for over two hours. Dorey repeatedly told him that if he went to the media about this, no one would believe either him or the reporter. Sharpe held up the three discs they'd taken from Ray Walker.

"What evidence do you have if you don't have these, Mr. Andrews?" Sharpe laughed, as he broke each disc into pieces in his hands.

Scott looks on helpless to do anything, but he knew they were right. Without any evidence, it would be his word against theirs, and the FAA and CIA would have total deniability; the agencies could say these cases, along with the JAL flight, never took place.

"All right, so I guess you guys win. I will not say a word to anyone about this. Now, may I please be united with my family? I just want us to go home alive and well."

"That's the proper attitude for you to have now, Scott. I will see to it that you and your family are taken back to Washington, DC, tomorrow. I will also call Stephen Clayton and let him know you will be ready to go back to work very soon," Dorey informed him.

Sharpe smiled, pleased in the knowledge that they had shut the door on this incident. He called for two guards to come and take Andrews back to his room.

Once they were alone in the office, Dorey told Sharpe his men were transferring Scott's ex-wife and daughter to a location just outside Hooper Bay, as he would be taking them back to DC in the morning. Dorey asked him about Ray Walker's fate.

"I have known Walker for over eight years and trained him myself. He is a very good operative for us to have, but his loyalty and intentions are not with us. He plans to expose us and our true agendas. We can't risk the effort he will make toward doing so. Tomorrow, he will be terminated, and his body will be cremated. No trail of Ray Walker will remain!" Sharpe replied.

Dorey agreed with the decision.

***

Just after 1:00 a.m., Billy Eagle and Nicole arrived at the home of
his good friend, James Counts, who was himself an amateur UFO
researcher. Billy asked Nicole for the remaining three discs so he
could show them to his friend. Nicole handed them over, and Billy
told her to stay in the truck and get some much-needed sleep, and
he would be done in about an hour.

CHAPTER 11

Ray was lying down on the small cot, impatiently waiting for the right moment to act. It had been over a half hour now since he'd heard any major sounds of movement on his floor. He knew he had to act now, as he was to be killed in a few hours. Ray bent down and ripped the small, plastic bag off his foot, tearing flesh off along with the hard surgical glue. He did the same with the right foot, then opened the bag with the wick and matches and inserted the wick into the bag of explosives. Ray quickly went over to the heavy steel door and placed the explosive bag right in between the door and its bottom hinge. He struck a match and lit the fuse then quickly shielded his face against the wall in the corner, as a loud explosion caused the door to break off both hinges and fly inward against the far wall. Smoke and flames shot over Ray's head, as he positioned himself against the entrance wall to hide.

**

Two guards came running into the room with their rifles still slung over their shoulders. Ray slammed one guard into the wall, as swept his leg low on the ground, taking the other man's feet out from beneath him. Ray made a double fist as he hit the same man in the face, causing his head to bounce off the hard floor. He grabbed the other man from behind and held his jaw with both hands; then he twisted the man's head hard to the left, snapping his neck instantly.

Ray quickly searched the guard's pockets and found a set of keys. Already knowing what the key to the handcuffs looked like, he opened them and then handcuffed the unconscious guard's hand to the hand of the dead guard.

Ray took the combat boots off the taller guard's feet, placed them on his own feet, and laced them up. He took both their rifles, slung one over his shoulder, and ran out through the flames around the door frame, heading for the control desk at the end of the hall. He overhead a siren, which alerted the base of an emergency on the third level. As the double doors started to open, Ray ducked down behind the desk. Five men rushed by him, trying to ascertain where the flames were coming from.

Ray looked up. Scanning the row of monitors on the desk, he was able to get a glimpse of what was on each level. He already knew what was on this level and that the labs where the alien testing was being done were housed on the fourth level. As he looked at the monitor showing the fifth level, he noticed more labs, but these rooms contained what appeared to be state-of-the-art weapons. He focused on the monitor showing the last level; the camera was facing a very large structure from the outside—from the ocean's view. Ray tried to zoom in on a very long object, which looked to be docked right under the last level to the base. But as the ocean was very dark and murky, Ray was unable to make out what the object was.

Ray cursed to himself as the double doors opened again and a few more men equipped with fire extinguishers ran passed him. He got up and ran through the doors before they closed on him.

***

Colonel Sharpe was in his private quarters getting changed into his uniform. He'd been awoken when the sirens went off.

Captain Harris called to inform him of Walker's escape.

"Chris, find him and terminate him on the spot! Have our men sweep all five levels in groups of four and search the oil rig. I will meet you on level three. Sharpe slammed his phone down and placed his pistol in his side holster. He grabbed his AR-15 rifle; headed out the door, where he was met by four armed men; and ran to the elevators.

＊

Ray was hiding in a small alcove as four men ran off the elevator and hurried past him. Ray quickly moved into the elevator before the doors closed. The car started to go down. As the car came to a stop on the fifth level, Ray bent down on one knee. As the doors opened, he fired in a burst of rounds at the four guards on the other side of the door, striking them in their heads and neck.

Ray quickly got to his feet and changed magazines; he looked around the dark hallway. He heard loud talking behind him. A voice said, "Kill him now," and Ray ran. He leaped through a large window, shattering the glass and landing hard on the floor. He didn't hesitate; he rolled on his back and fired at the men as they came through the door to the room. His rounds struck them in the lower legs, and the two men fell to the floor. Ray fired at the two guards who came through the door, and his rounds found their mark. As they dropped dead, Ray rose to his feet and looked around the office. He noticed computers and lab equipment, along with what looked like state-of-the-art machinery that seemed to be for manufacturing some kind of engine or propulsion system.

One of the men who Ray had shot in the legs was on the floor screaming in pain. Ray went over and kicked the man's rifle away from him then kicked the man to turn him over so he was face up.

"Now if you want to live, tell me what they are doing on this level and what the structure below us in the ocean is," Ray growled.

The man screamed in pain, took a long breath and then answered Ray. "On this level, they are retrofitting advanced engine systems with the captured craft a few years ago, along with modifying our modern weapons, using their advanced weapons." He begged Ray not to kill him.

Ray looked around the room and then back at the guard. "Who are *they*?" Ray demanded.

"The grays—the large grays. Sharpe is on orders from the CIA to find out what makes them so advanced in comparison to humans—so we can find their weaknesses and defeat them."

Ray thought about what this man had just said and then back to what Colonel Sharpe had told him about the big firefight with the grays at the Dulce Base in New Mexico.

The guard stopped breathing and closed his eyes as he died from loss of blood.

Ray was about to look around the room for paperwork or discs that documented the work the guard had told him about—evidence that could expose what was going on—when gunfire erupted behind him. A round struck Ray in his left arm, and he flew off his feet and landed next to a large countertop. He low crawled behind the counter to give himself cover, just as five men burst into the room and Captain Chris Harris yelled out to kill Walker now.

Ray pulled his jacket off and checked the wound on his arm; the round had grazed his left bicep but caused a severe gash. Ray scanned his immediate area and found a towel. He ripped it down the middle and fastened a tourniquet to stop the bleeding, using the other piece of towel to wipe away the blood.

A guard rounded the corner, and Ray kicked an office chair on wheels hard at him. When the chair stopped the guard's progress, Ray aimed his rifle and shot him in the head. Ray quickly leaped to the fallen body. Grasping the guard's AR-15 in his hands, Ray turned and fired rapidly at two more guards, who fired their weapons but missed Ray, as he was lying on the floor.

His rounds found their mark, and the guards dropped to the floor dead. Ray crawled under the counter and came out the other side. Now behind the fourth guard, he rose to his feet and fired directly into the back of the guard's head. As the man flew forward off his feet and fell dead, Harris yelled in anger, aimed, and shot. Ray moved quickly, leaping into the air and diving behind a countertop. The rounds shattered the glass tubes and computers, and glass rained down all around Ray. He prepared to fire at Harris, but his rifle jammed. While jumping to avoid the previous rounds, he'd slammed the barrel into the floor, damaging it.

Harris was about to shoot. Ray hurled his rifle at Harris, knocking the pistol out of his hand. Ray made a leaping tackle, and both men tumbled to the ground. Harris reached down and took out his long KA-BAR knife. Ray looked up and saw the blade coming towards his face. He rolled to his right side to avoid the blade. Harris got to his feet and lunged at Ray, knife first. Ray spun around, again dodging the blade. Then he reached back and grabbed Harris's hand, flinging his assailant to the floor.

Harris lost the knife. As he tried to reach for it, Ray kicked him hard in the ribs again and again. Harris grabbed Ray's foot and pulled him down to the floor, and the two men began pounding one another's faces with closed fists. Ray was able to block an incoming punch and then land one to Harris's nose, dead center, breaking it instantly. Blood poured from each nostril. Harris fell on his back, reached for his pistol, and shot up to a sitting position, ready to fire. Ray threw the knife at his opponent, hard and fast. The blade plunged into Harris's left eye and pierced his brain; he fell dead.

Ray jumped to his feet, grabbed a fully loaded rifle and pulled the knife out of Harris's skull. He ran out of the room and down the hallway, stopping at the elevators so he could think about what to do next. He wanted to see what was below level five. He stepped into the elevator and pressed the last button, which was unmarked.

The doors closed behind him, and the elevator started its slow descent. When it came to a stop, the doors opened very slowly, and Ray cautiously peered out to discover that he was in a connecting pressurized airlock with thick, clear, acrylic windows, which led to a dark, very thick door. Ray stepped out in the hallway but used his knife to keep the elevator doors propped open. He crept toward the door, his rifle at the ready. Arriving at the door, he reached out and touched it. It was very cold to the touch and felt like a hard aluminum metal of sorts—one Ray knew he had encountered a few times before.

All of a sudden, the door slid open. Ray came face-to-face with a very tall being. He stumbled backward trying to get away from the large gray alien.

The alien let out a piercing shrieking sound, which echoed loudly in the small airlock. The alien pointed his wrist in Ray's direction. Ray anticipated what was coming, and he dropped to the floor as a bright blue plasma beam shot from a weapon attached to the being's wrist. Missing its target, the hot beam hit the acrylic glass causing it to crack. Ray sat up and shot at the being. A round hit the being's shoulder, and it fell backward as another alien appeared in the doorway.

Ray knew he couldn't fight them all off. He cursed out loud and fired his rifle at the spot where the glass wall was damaged. As his rounds broke the glass, the ocean water started to pour into the airlock. Ray got to his feet and jumped back into the elevator. He removed the knife, and as the doors closed, he watched the beings help the one he'd wounded get back into the craft.

Shaken up by what he had just seen, Ray knew now he couldn't allow this place to remain operational. He pressed the button that would take him to the top level of the platform; he had to get to his bag that contained the explosives.

***

At the security desk, an alarm went off to alert the crew of the structural damage to the now flooding airlock. Colonel Sharpe ran to the desk, his guards in tow. The security officers briefed him on what was happening. Stunned to learn that their high-tech base was in danger of floating into the ocean floor, Sharpe yelled into the radio, directing all units to stay away from level six.

Just then, Carlos Dorey appeared, running toward the security desk. With him were five guards and Scott Andrews in plastic wrist restraints. Sharpe filled him in on what was happening.

"Sharpe, my team and I are flying to Hooper Bay now. And we are taking Andrews with us. If you are unable to contain Walker and we lose the whole facility, you know what I have been ordered to do!"

"Yes, I understand! Hurry; the helicopter is ready for you!" Sharpe ordered.

Dorey and his CIA agents headed to the second set of elevators and the helicopter that would take them back to the mainland.

As they left, Sharpe was informed that his second in command, Captain Chris Harris, had been found dead, along with many soldiers, on the fifth level.

"That damn Walker; how many men do we have left?" Sharpe asked his first sergeant.

"Eighteen, sir," the sergeant responded.

Sharpe cursed in response, watching the airlock on the monitor in front of him, which was now totally filled with water. The grays' craft released itself from the airlock as it broke apart and collapsed into the ocean.

The base's head engineer came forward and told Sharpe that, now that the airlock had been destroyed, there was nothing to keep the water from seeping into the elevator shaft; in only an hour, all lower levels would be flooded, and eventually, the structures would buckle and collapse.

"Look, have ten men destroy all the lab work and experiments on level four and gather all discs and paperwork, along with the remaining scientists, and get them to the last helicopter. I will take eight men and kill Walker myself; I will call Dorey and let him know we lost control here. We only have a little time left to make it to the last boat that's docked topside. So let's move, men!" Sharpe ordered.

The men broke into two groups.

As Sharpe and his group of men ran into the elevators, he took out his cell phone and called Carlos Dorey; Dorey's team was about to lift off from the platform. Sharpe told him that the levels below would be submerged from all the damage to the airlock and that the grays' craft has detached itself in preparation to leave soon.

"Oh my God, Mike, we can't let the whole world know about this! I will call CIA Director John Crawford and inform him about this now. He will then give the order to have the platform canceled all together!" Dorey replied.

Sharpe told Dorey that his people were gathering all traces of their work and evidence and that he would make sure Walker was dead.

***

Dorey hung up on Sharpe and placed the call to his boss.

Sitting behind Dorey, Scott listened to all that was happening and just shook his head in anger.

"So this is how you and your people operate. Whatever it takes to make sure this 'never happened'; the decisions are easy for you—no matter the cost of human lives. All that matters is keeping this all a big secret," Scott yelled.

"That's right, Mr. Andrews. And as a top-level FAA executive, you should thank your lucky stars that you and your family were allowed to live!" Dorey shouted back at him.

Then turned from Scott and began talking to his boss, Director Crawford, on the phone.

***

As Ray stepped onto the rig's platform level, he saw a helicopter flying toward Hooper Bay. He quickly made his way over to the cabinet where he had stored his explosives. Just then, he heard a thunderous explosion and felt a shockwave beneath his feet. Ray realized that the order must have been given to destroy all the experiments and work to cover this location up. He retrieved his bag with the Claymore mine and the remaining three glow stick explosives. As he was about to turn around, gunfire roared behind him. He leaped out of the way, and the rounds hit the metal cabinet. Crawling fast on the platform floor in search of cover, he looked up and noticed three men coming toward him.

Hiding behind one of the support columns, he quickly lit one of the glow sticks.

A voice ordered the men to box him in now.

Ray looked over his right shoulder, as he flung the glow stick at the men. It exploded in the air, and the flash fire streaks consumed two of the men. As they were set on fire, they screamed in horrific pain. Ray turned and fired his rifle, striking them down.

Sharpe quickly fired back. Ray returned to the safety of the column, and Sharpe's rounds struck the heavy steel support beam. Ray dropped the rifle, which was out of rounds. Taking the AR-15 rifle from his shoulder, he dashed to the next support beam before Sharpe and his remaining guards could aim at him. Their rounds struck the metal grate beneath his feet. Ray looked back, took aim, and fired as he leaped into the air. His round hit a guard dead in his eyes. Ray slammed into the column with his left shoulder. The force of the impact caused him to let go of his rifle, and it flew into the sea. Ray landed on his back. The pain tore throughout his whole left arm, aggravating the flesh wound he'd received earlier.

Ray opened the assault pack; he had to get the last explosives ready while Sharpe was changing magazines. He lit the last two glow stick as the elevator doors opened and the remaining five guards stepped out onto the platform. Ray stood up and heaved the sticks at them. Sharpe ordered them to take cover. The sticks exploded in the elevator car, killing three of the men instantly. The other two were propelled through the air. One landed in the ocean, and the other landed just a few feet away from Ray. Moving in behind the stunned guard, Ray grabbed his head and smashed it into the steel column repeatedly. Blood flew from the open gash. Ray threw the man's body into the water.

Sharpe ran over to him and smacked Ray in his injured shoulder with the butt of his rifle. As Ray fell to the steel deck, Sharpe kicked him in the ribs repeatedly. Then he bent down and picked Ray's head up and hit him square in the face. As the last guard was pulling himself from the water onto the deck, Sharpe picked up Ray's assault pack and looked inside.

"Impressive, Walker—a Claymore mine. This gives me a great idea," Sharpe said. He turned to his man and ordered him to set off the Claymore in the last operational elevator shaft, saying that the explosion would fracture the acrylic glass, causing a massive flood in the remaining shaft and collapsing the lower levels even more quickly. Sharpe then ordered the guard to go and have the jet boat on the west dock ready for them to leave. He would deal with Mr. Walker.

The man rushed away with the mine.

Holding his injured shoulder, which he knew was either dislocated or fractured, Ray crawled away.

Sharpe stared down at him and smiled. "Well, Ray, it doesn't appear to me that the hero wins this battle in the end!" He kicked Ray again, this time square in the face; blood shot out of his mouth.

Ray turned over on his back, expecting Sharpe to shoot him, but Sharpe just dropped his rifle.

They felt the explosion from the mine. Then Sharpe yelled to his man, saying he'd be right there, to get the boat ready for their departure.

"Soon, Ray, the jet fighters will be here from Eielson Air Force Base to destroy what's left of the oil rig! Of course, the media will receive the cover story that a fire within the rig itself caused the explosion. And no traces of what really went on here will remain!" Sharpe yelled.

Ray looked at his former colonel, holding his left shoulder.

"You really did a job here, Ray; only you could have completed this kind of a suicide mission alone—because I trained you!" Sharpe threw his rifle into the water.

Ray knew what Sharpe had in mind.

Sharpe pulled out his long KA-BAR knife and motioned for Ray to stand up. "Come on, Ray! My simply shooting you wouldn't be a fair way to end this. Let me find out how well I really trained you!"

Ray removed his knife from his side sheath and held it in his right hand. As he looked into Sharpe's eyes, he thought of all the man had put him through. "Come on, you son of a bitch!" Ray yelled over a roaring crash, as the steel framework of the levels beneath them collapsed and broke apart into the Bering Sea.

Sharpe rushed at Ray, swinging his knife wildly. Ray twisted his body around, and the blade just missed him.

Ray came at Sharpe. They clung together ferociously. Both men separated and swung at each other again. Sharpe thrust up and down rapidly, and his blade caught Ray on his right wrist, cutting him deeply. Blood shot from the wound and Ray cursed in pain. Sharpe told him to be a man and deal with the pain.

With Ray's injured left shoulder, Sharpe had the advantage. Anger filled Ray as Sharpe rushed at him again. Ray braced himself, fell to one leg, and swept Sharpe's legs out from under him. Sharpe fell to the iron plate; Ray leaped to his feet and kicked Sharpe in his back again and again. Sharpe turned over and made it to his feet. Ray backed up as Sharpe swung rapidly at his face. Ray moved out of the way and sliced Sharpe across his left thigh, coming up fast with the blade and slicing Sharpe across his chest.

Sharpe moved back, but Ray didn't hesitate. He rushed at his opponent. But Sharpe kicked him in his knee and threw a hard punch to his jaw, stunning him and causing him to drop his knife. Sharpe swung and struck Ray across his right shoulder.

As Ray fell to the platform, Sharpe looked down at him and smiled. "I guess you're not as strong as I am, huh, Walker!" Sharpe snarled. He lunged at Ray with his knife, as Ray lay helpless on his back.

Ray moved to his left side. He reached for his knife and thrust it hard into Sharpe's left side as the colonel fell on top of him. As Sharpe screamed in pain, Ray shoved the knife in deeper. Blood poured out all over Ray's knife and hand. Ray yelled back. "Maybe I'm not stronger, but I'm faster!"

Sharpe closed his eyes and died. Ray pushed the colonel's body off himself and took Sharpe's sidearm pistol from its holster. He ran toward the jet boat that was waiting for Sharpe. Jumping into the boat, the soldier announced, without looking up, that they could leave now.

Ray held the pistol to the back of his head, and the soldier looked back at Ray in shock.

"Yes, we can go now! Full speed to the docks of Hooper Bay!" Ray ordered.

The soldier moved the throttle into drive, and they speed off toward Hooper Bay. Ray kept a sharp eye on the soldier as he tended to the two deep gashes he'd received in the knife battle with Sharpe.

All of a sudden, there was a large disturbance in the water behind them. Ray looked back. A massive, dark craft ejected itself out of the ocean waters and hovered in midair for a few moments. As Ray and the other man watched in amazement, the oval-shaped craft darted up into the atmosphere at an incredibly fast speed until they could no longer see it in the daybreak sky of early morning.

Ray broke into a quiet smile when, all of a sudden, two F-16 fighter jets flew overhead and fired four heat-seeking missiles at the platform. It exploded into a massive fireball; flames and smoke bellowed amid an earth-shattering boom, and a huge plume of smoke rose into the air.

Ray just watched and shook his head. "There goes all the evidence," he said and cursed, remembering that he'd left the three discs in his bag.

He instructed the soldier to drive the boat to the far end of the boating dock, which was less populated. He didn't want any civilians to see them. The sun was rising behind them, as the time was now 7:00 a.m.

***

Carlos Dorey had received word that the platform and the concealed lower levels had been destroyed. The CIA would intercept all media reports, and the cover story would be that a faulty pipe system had caused a massive explosion and that there was no oil spill to worry about. Dorey waited on the banks of the dock, along with his men and Scott Andrews. A second helicopter landed nearby.

Scott watched as four armed men climbed out of the helicopter, followed by Kimberly and Alexandra. Scott's hands were freed from the ties. Alexandra ran to Scott and hugged him tightly. Kimberly followed and embraced them all together, and Dorey ordered his men to lower their weapons.

Scott asked them if they were all right and said that he was very sorry for all of this. Kimberly replied that she and Alexandra had been treated well; she just hoped it was all over with now.

Just as Dorey was about to speak, one of his men told them to look at the incoming boat. They raised their rifles as they spotted Ray Walker in the boat with his pistol pointing right at them.

Scott and his family watched in shock, sure the agents were about to open fire at him. But Dorey ordered his men to hold fire and let the boat dock. It came to a stop. Ray fixed his eyes, filled with hatred, on Dorey, as he climbed up onto the dock and walked very slowly toward the small crowd. Ray was utterly exhausted and suffering blood loss from the deep gashes he'd received during all the fighting. Dorey told his men to be ready, as he stepped forward to confront Walker.

"My goodness, Mr. Walker, how did you manage to escape and destroy our billion-dollar facility all by yourself?" Dorey asked.

Ray smiled. "My former lead commander taught me very well, and now he is your former lead commander of whatever bases or top secret projects you still have planned!"

Learning of Colonel Sharpe's death, Dorey became very angry. "We recovered the three discs you and that reporter made along with Mr. Andrews here! I want the remaining discs you have," he snarled. "And then I will let you all go free because all this never happened!"

Kimberly whispered to Scott, urging him to do whatever Dorey asked so they could go free. Scott whispered back that he didn't have any discs or any more evidence with him.

"I did have three discs on me," Ray roared back at Dorey. "But they were lost in the explosion, as I forgot them on the platform. You can search me and my friends. I know I don't have anything linking to all of this. So you and the CIA, along with the Air Force, are in the clear once again, Mr. Dorey!"

Behind them, a vehicle quickly drove up, and they all turned their attention to it. The agents shifted, pointing their weapons at the large SUV.

Nicole got out, along with Billy Eagle. As Eagle pointed his shotgun at Dorey's men, Nicole ran over and hugged Ray tightly.

Eagle yelled at Dorey, "Just hold on a second; we have some dealing to do."

"What would you have that is of any importance to me and this whole event Mr. …?" Dorey asked.

Nicole reached inside her jacket and took out the three additional discs that Ray had made.

As Ray looked on in shock, Nicole pinches him softly on the back.

"Here! Now you have all the copies we made! I can't say a word about this to anyone or write a story about this if I don't have any evidence. You know that!" Nicole yelled.

Dorey reached out and took the discs from Nicole.

"All right, Carlos, you have everything you want now!" Scott said. "Let all of us go, including Ray! You can't kill him if I'm going to return to the FAA and Nicole to *The Washington Times*."

Dorey looked back at Ray Walker, and they give each other a long, deep stare. "All right, you have yourself a deal then, Miss Martone. Even if you print a word about this, no one will ever believe you! And, Mr. Walker, I just hope you stay out of my way in the future! Because next time I will not be so forgiving!" Dorey yelled.

With that, he told his men to load up in the helicopters, they were done here.

Ray and the others watched. The wind kicked up dust in their faces from the heavy spinning of the helicopter's rotor blades as the agents lifted off and headed back toward Anchorage.

Ray turned and held Nicole's face gently as he gave her a deep kiss.

Scott looked on for a moment. Then he said, "What the hell!" and embraced Kimberly, kissing her tenderly.

Alexandra hugged her parents, and Billy Eagle looked on and smiled.

"I hate to break this all up, people, but I think we should get going now!" he finally said.

Stunned by Ray's injuries, Nicole told Billy Eagle that they would go directly to the emergency room of the closest hospital. They all climbed into Billy's SUV.

Ray sat in the front passenger seat, while Scott, his family, and Nicole road in the two backseats. Billy gave Ray a clean towel to cover the wound on his shoulder, which was still bleeding. As Ray applied pressure to the wound, he looked back at Nicole and asked why she'd pinched him.

"Show them," she told Billy.

He held up five discs copies he'd made with the help of his friend.

As Ray and Scott started to laugh, Nicole told them she would be writing this big story after all and holding a major press conference to tell the world of the events that had taken place.

CHAPTER 12

It had been three days since the events in Alaska had taken place. Stephen Clayton was about to enter his office. His secretary stopped him and informed him that Scott Andrews was in his office waiting to talk to him. Clayton looked at her in surprise. He instructed her to hold all calls and that he would take no visitors, that this meeting with Scott was very important.

He walked into his office. As he entered, he saw Scott seated and dressed in a full suit. Scott rose from the chair to greet Clayton. Both men smiled at one another and shook hands.

"My God, Scott, you're alive and well! Welcome home! How is your family? Are they all right?" Clayton asked, concerned.

"We are all good, thank you. I'm sure you know what happened to Susan Morrow and why I was up in Alaska for as long as I was."

"Yes, Scott, I know about Susan, and I'm sorry. But like you, I was forced into the position, as head administrator for the FAA, to see that this encounter with a civilian airliner could not affect the world and our skies. I agreed with the CIA that secrecy was the best protocol when it came to the knowledge that beings from other worlds exist."

Scott simply listened to what Clayton was telling him. Be he couldn't accept how the FAA head felt. "So hiding the truth about this and sending me all the way up there to investigate this whole matter, knowing damn well that I would be served a bunch of lies, lying to me yourself—that seemed like the best protocol?" Scott demanded. "I learned the truth through Susan and one of her best friends, a reporter. That led us to try to uncover this whole thing and resulted in Susan being murdered, along with countless others! Besides that, my own family was almost killed off because we tried to do what we thought was right!"

"Look, Scott, you and Susan were both in the position to not get involved here—even when you both found out the truth about the voice tapes and the radar confirmation of the UFO. But you both still went ahead as if uncovering the true facts was some kind of a cloak and dagger game! I'm not responsible for what happened to you and, most of all, Susan! So you better accept that. Keep your mouth shut about this whole ordeal if you want your job back, my friend," Clayton warned. He was prepared to terminate Scott's position with the FAA if he had to.

Scott reached into his jacket pocket and took out a sealed envelope. He handed it to Clayton with his left hand and made a fist with his right hand. Swinging very hard, he punched Clayton right in the jaw. The FAA head fell back into the chair behind him and onto the floor.

"That's my letter of resignation, Stephen! One of my staffers will gather up the things in my office and have them shipped to me. Sorry for hitting you, but that's for Susan and for how I feel you handled this whole thing!" Scott called, as he turned and walked out the door.

Clayton's secretary looked at her boss on the floor; she rushed over to help him. Stephen held his aching jaw. She asked if he wanted her to call the police and report Scott for assaulting him. Clayton told her no, just to let him go and inform personnel that

Scott Andrews had resigned from the FAA.

Scott made his way to the parking lot, where Kimberly and Alexandra were waiting for him at their car. Kimberly asked him if he was all right, and Scott told her he was fine.

"It's over; we can all go home now," Scott told them, as he and Kimberly kissed each other.

"Back to the house?" Alexandra asked.

"Yes, sweetheart, back home to our apartment to pack our things, and then to New York." New York was where the Andrews family—reunited again—had originally come from.

***

The entire media was in high anticipation of the press conference that would begin any moment in Washington, DC, at the National Press Club, following the breaking news article Nicole Martone had written for *The Washington Times*. The articled had explained a cover-up of a UFO encounter with cargo jet JAL 1628 on October 17 of this year.

Nicole had already done two exclusive news interviews with the pilot, Joe Hiroki, and former FAA executive in charge of investigating the case, Scott Andrews. The story took the entire world by storm, as both Hiroki and Andrews had explained the former's witnessing of the amazing UFOs that tracked his aircraft. Andrews had noted that it was the first time the FAA, along with military and civilian radar, had confirmation of not one but three UFOs for over fifty minutes.

Besides the many media members who were filming and taking pictures of the news conference, everyone who was involved in the event would be in attendance.

Now they were all seated on stage in a row, ready to explain their side of the events as they'd experienced them. The host finished the introductions; he'd introduced each guest, including Scott Andrews, pilot Joe Hiroki and his flight team, and Nicole Martone. But one seat remained empty. Ray Walker had not yet appeared for the conference.

Ray had talked to Nicole the night before and promised her he would come and talk.

As the host finished talking, Scott Andrews took center stage at the podium. He introduced himself and explained his former position with the FAA. He looked into the crowd of people and saw Kimberly and Alexandra smiling at him, proud of him for having the courage to come forward and speak. Scott also saw FAA Administrator Stephen Clayton, and sitting next to him was CIA operative Carlos Dorey. They were very interested in what was to be discussed during the conference.

***

Two hours into the conference, Scott and Hiroki and his flight team had completed their statements. Nicole was now beginning to tell the audience about her involvement in the whole ordeal. She told them that none of the evidence would have been possible without the help and great courage of former military operative Ray Walker. All of a sudden, a set of double doors opened up, and Ray walked into the room wearing a fine, dark blue suit and tie and holding a folder. It contained his prepared statement he was about to tell the world, detailing his work as a deep military operative dealing with classified UFO and alien events. Nicole smiled at him as he made his way to the stage. Ray walked up and took his seat. Scott shook his hand, as he sat beside him.

When Nicole was done talking, she introduced Ray Walker to everyone. The crowd stood up and gave him a standing ovation. Ray walked up to Nicole. They hugged, and he kissed her on the cheek.

"Just don't be nervous and you will do just fine," Nicole told him before she walked back and took her seat.

As everyone stopped clapping and took their seats, Ray introduced himself. He explained how he'd been picked, along with other Army Special Forces operatives, to be part of a top secret team assigned to deal with alien beings and crashed saucers from other worlds. He noted that the military had known of the existence of aliens way before the Roswell Incident happened. He talked about how he'd dealt with three recovered saucers with his team and how Colonel Michael Sharpe had trained him.

Ray then explained why he was disgusted by having all this kept in the dark from not only the American public but from the whole world. It was, after all, the biggest discovery of humankind. Earth was not alone as the existing planet of life in the entire universe.

Nicole had tears in her eyes as she listened to Ray's moving speech.

When the press conference was over, Ray and Scott spoke individually with reporters, a host of cameras trained on each. They explained that they would talk more in depth about this famous case as guests on a variety of talk shows. Scott mentioned that he planned to write a book about his experiences, detailing how he'd gone from being a complete skeptic when it came to UFOs and aliens to being a complete believer.

One reporter asked Ray when he would be giving his first exclusive, tell-all interview. Ray hugged Nicole, who was standing next to him, and said, "The first interview I give will be with my future wife!" With that, he and Nicole kissed each other.

***

The next morning, Carlos Dorey was called to meet with CIA Director John Crawford. As Dorey opened the thick door to the office, he caught Crawford's eyes, which showed both anger and frustration. Dorey closed the door and sat directly in front of Crawford's large, wooden desk.

"Tell me, Carlos, besides the discs containing the voice and radar findings of the plane and UFO, was there any video footage of the craft or any EBE life forms in their possession?" Crawford questioned.

"No, just the fire of the platform after we had it destroyed," Dorey replied.

Relief crossed Crawford's face. "So after all that we have been through with this event, with the exception of those discs and the testimony of the witnesses themselves, we still have full deniability of everything?"

"Correct, sir, they can play their tapes and radar footage all they want in the media. But they still don't have one changeable piece of evidence that proves the grays exist or to prove the validity of any other famous cases over the years, which have come to be only urban legends," Dorey answered.

"So where did the craft go, if I may ask, sir?" Dorey raised his eyebrows.

Crawford rose from his desk and held the remote control for the large LCD viewing screen behind his desk. He brought up a large map of Alaska and zoomed in on the city of Deadhorse. "I had our satellite operators track the craft once it left its location in the Bering Sea. We tracked it to the Arctic Ocean, where it submerged once again about fifty miles north of Deadhorse. We still don't know if the grays are willing to work with us again or if their intentions are hostile toward all humans, as they seemed to be in New Mexico in 1979."

"So I guess we will try and make contact with them again, sir?"

Crawford told him that, yes, he had ordered their black ops team to take a submarine and try to reestablish communication with the grays. "So we should know something by this time tomorrow."

Dorey nodded and then asked his next question. "And if they do become hostile? What do we do then?"

"Then God help us all," Crawford answered. He was uncertain of the future relationship between humankind and the aliens, and he was uncertain of the grays' true agenda here on Earth.

ABOUT THE AUTHOR

Mark Barresi spent three years in the army infantry, training at Fort Benning and then Fort Campbell, where he expanded his military knowledge and skills while going to college and taking creative writing courses. He has followed the paths of his favorite established authors, James Byron Huggins and Clive Cussler, and has authored seven books establishing himself as one of the great new talents of the action and horror genre. *Encounter Over Alaska* will be made into a major movie, based on the true UFO case of Japanese Jetliner JAL1628 that encountered three massive UFOs while flying over Alaska in November 1986. Barresi made a guest appearance on the History Channel's hit show *Pawn Stars* in 2014. He enjoys traveling, collecting antiques and being an animal rights activist, caring for abused and neglected animals. He plans to write his next novel *The Encounter Within Alaska* in the near future. He currently lives in New York City.